CLAIMING HIS WEDDING NIGHT CONSEQUENCE

CLAIMING HIS WEDDING NIGHT CONSEQUENCE

ABBY GREEN

MILLS & BOON

First published in Great Britain 2018
by Mills & Boon, an imprint of HarperCollins*Publishers*
1 London Bridge Street, London, SE1 9GF

Large Print edition 2019

© 2018 Abby Green

ISBN: 978-0-263-07884-8

MIX
Paper from
responsible sources
FSC™ C007454

This book is produced from independently certified FSC™ paper to ensure responsible forest management. For more information visit www.harpercollins.co.uk/green.

Printed and bound in Great Britain
by CPI Group (UK) Ltd, Croydon, CR0 4YY

This is for Franca Poli,
for all of her wonderful support
and very generous help.
Grazie! X

CHAPTER ONE

'I AM VERY sorry to be the bearer of such bad news, Signorina Caruso, but the fact is that your father had borrowed for years to keep the castello afloat and the bank is threatening to take possession of it now, unless you can buy it back at market value—which I'm afraid is impossible, considering the lack of funds in your family bank account...'

Chiara stood at the huge window of the drawing room where she'd had a meeting with the family solicitor after her parents' double funeral just a couple of days before. Her arms were wrapped around herself as if that might offer some comfort.

For the last two days and sleepless nights the words had swirled in her head in a confusing painful jumble: *bank, take possession, lack of funds.* And she was no nearer to seeing a way out of this mess that didn't end up with her losing everything.

The family *castello* was an imposing centuries-old castle, set dramatically on the southern coastline of Sicily. Prime real estate that had once functioned and thrived as a farm, growing and exporting lemons and olives. Staples of Italian agriculture.

But once the recession had hit, and the market had taken a nosedive, their crops had all but dried up and died due to lack of demand. They couldn't afford to keep staff on and, while her father had done his best, clearly it hadn't been enough. Chiara had offered help time and time again, but her father—old-fashioned and conservative—hadn't deemed it 'appropriate work' for a girl. And she hadn't realised just how much he'd been borrowing to keep their heads above water.

She castigated herself now. She *should* have known. But her mother had been ill with cancer, and Chiara had been preoccupied with caring for her. The only reason Chiara was alive today and her father wasn't was because he'd decided to take his wife to her weekly chemotherapy appointment at the hospital in Calabria.

That morning a week ago he had said to Chiara, *'You need to go down to the village and see if you can get a job. It's not enough to just care for your mother any more.'*

His tone had been sharp. He'd never made any secret of the fact that he was disappointed Chiara hadn't been a boy, and that after suffering complications with Chiara's birth her mother hadn't been able to have any more children.

So Chiara had gone down to the village—to find that there were no jobs available. She'd never been more aware of her lack of qualifications, and the looks she'd received from the locals had made her feel paranoid.

As a child she'd been sickly, so her mother had home-schooled her. But even when she'd recovered and become strong they'd kept her at the *castello.* Her father had always had a paranoia about privacy and security, forbidding Chiara to bring anyone back to the *castello*—not that she'd had any friends! And then her mother had fallen ill, and Chiara had become her carer.

After humiliating herself in the village, looking for work, Chiara had returned home to find her parents still not returned from the hospital.

So she'd gone down to her secret place—a small beach tucked out of sight of the *castello*—and indulged in her favourite pastime, daydreaming, unaware that her parents were breathing their last in a tangle of metal after a catastrophic car crash.

What had made her feel even guiltier afterwards was the dream she'd indulged in—the same one she'd always had: leaving the *castello* and travelling the world. Meeting a handsome man and finding love and excitement. Yearning for...*more*.

Now Chiara's guilty sense of entrapment mocked her. She was finally free, but at such a cost that it left her breathless. She'd lost both her parents, and now it would appear she was about to lose the only home she'd ever known.

It was at a time like this that she felt her isolation even more keenly. Chiara had always lamented her lack of siblings, and had promised herself from an early age that she would have a large family one day. She never wanted any child of hers to feel as alone as she had, in spite of her mother's love and affection which had never quite made up for her father's disappointment.

Except now, if the bank took possession of the

castello, the least of her worries would be a sense of isolation. She'd have much bigger concerns. Where would she go? What would she do? Her fruitless search for a job in the village was surely the tip of the iceberg when it came to finding work.

The truth was that she wasn't prepared for life beyond the *castello* walls at all. In spite of her dreams, she'd always counted on the *castello* being the anchor of her life, so that no matter where she went or what she did it would always be there to come back to. And eventually—some day—she'd hoped to fill it with a loving family.

The thought of having to leave her home now was agonising...and more than terrifying.

She felt a nudge at her leg and looked down to see their ancient family dog, Spiro, a Sicilian Shepherd. Shaggy and big. He looked up at her with mournful eyes and whined. He'd melted Chiara's heart when he was a pup, almost fifteen years ago, the runt of the litter and almost blind.

Chiara stroked his head and murmured soft words, wondering what on earth she would do with Spiro when she had to leave.

Just then she heard a noise coming from outside,

and Spiro tensed and let out a feeble-sounding bark. Chiara looked out of the window to see a very sleek silver sports car prowling its way up the drive. The automatic main gates had stopped functioning years ago, in spite of her father's attempts to fix them.

Belatedly she recalled the solicitor saying something the other day about a businessman who had a proposition to put to her. She'd barely taken it in at the time, too overwhelmed with all the other news. But this could be the man he'd been talking about.

The car drew to a halt in the main courtyard, which suddenly looked very shabby and rundown next to such gleaming perfection. Feeling a spurt of irritation that a complete stranger thought it would be okay to discuss anything just days after a funeral, Chiara made reassuring noises to Spiro and then turned from the window and went through the *castello* to the main door, fully intending to tell whoever it was to come back on a more suitable day.

She doused the feeling of panic that there might not *be* a more suitable day. She had no idea how fast banks acted in this scenario when taking possession. She could be tossed out by the end of the week.

Feeling more vulnerable and raw than she'd ever felt in her life, Chiara pulled open the massive oak door. For a second she was blinded by sunlight, so all she had was an impression of a very tall dark shape climbing the steps.

She was about to put her hand over her eyes to shade them when the visitor stepped into her eyeline, blocking the sun with his height. Chiara blinked, and blinked again, her hand dropping to her side ineffectually as she took in the sight before her.

It was a man. But such a man as she'd never seen before. The kind of man she'd only seen in her fantasies or read about in stories.

Thick black hair, slightly messy, framed the most savagely beautiful face Chiara had ever seen. High cheekbones and an aquiline nose lent it more than a hint of regality, and his tall, proud bearing reinforced the impression. His mouth was as sculpted as the rest of him—firm and strong.

An intriguing air of decadent sensuality and steeliness made a quiver of something very feminine go through Chiara, all the way to the centre of her being.

She struggled to rouse herself out of the strange lethargy that seemed to have taken hold of her, hindering her ability to function. 'I'm sorry… can I help you?'

The man's eyes narrowed on her and Chiara saw they were a very dark brown—and totally unreadable. Something cool slid down her spine and she unconsciously felt for Spiro's reassuring presence behind her, even though he was so old and blind he was totally ineffectual as a guard dog.

The man looked emotionless, but Chiara sensed something almost volcanic under the surface and it was very intimidating. Strangely, though, she didn't fear for her safety. It was a much more ambiguous fear. A fear for something deep within her that was coming to life…*desire.*

'I am here to see Chiara Caruso. Maybe you would be so kind as to fetch your mistress for me.'

His voice was deep and gravelly, tugging on Chiara's senses. He hadn't posed it as a question. She realised that he must think she was the housekeeper. They'd let the housekeeper go a long time ago. Hence the general air of decay and dishevelment in and around the *castello*. But, effectively, she *was* now the housekeeper, so it was silly to feel something shrivel up inside her that he might assume her to be menial staff.

She was very aware of her plain black mourning dress, make-up free face, and long unruly hair. She knew she was no great beauty, with her unfashionably full figure and average height.

She tipped up her chin. '*I* am Chiara Caruso.'

His eyes narrowed even more and a look of sheer incredulity crossed his face. 'You?'

Tension and self-consciousness stiffened Chiara's whole body. 'I'm not sure exactly what you were expecting but, yes, I can assure you that I'm Chiara Caruso. Who, may I ask, are *you*?'

Those eyes seemed to get even colder, if that was possible. 'I am Nicolo Santo Domenico.'

He seemed to be waiting for some kind of response—as if his name should mean something. But it didn't.

Chiara prompted, 'And...? How can I help you?'

Confirming her suspicion, he said, 'You don't know who I am?'

Chiara felt bewildered now. 'Should I?'

The man emitted a sound like an incredulous laugh. 'You're seriously expecting me to believe you don't know who I am?'

The man's arrogance was astounding!

Chiara took her hand off the door and folded her arms across her chest. 'No, I don't know who you are. Now, if you have nothing better to do than interrogate me on my own doorstep then I'll ask you to leave. We had a funeral here this week—it is not an appropriate time.'

His eyes gleamed. 'To the contrary...now is the *most* appropriate time for this conversation. May I?'

He sidestepped her neatly and was walking into the vast stone hallway before she could stop him.

Spiro whined and Chiara whirled around. 'Excuse me, what on *earth* do you think you're doing? This is my property!'

Except it's not really, reminded a little voice.

The man turned around to face her and Chiara got the full impact of him. It was almost too much. He made the majestic reception area seem small. He had to be well over six feet, and broad with it. He wore a dark suit that could only be custom-made as it clung to his well-honed physique like a second skin. His air of intense physicality made Chiara think of bare-knuckle fighters she'd seen in a documentary once. It was as if his suit was just a flimsy concession to urbanity.

His gaze slid down to beside Chiara and his lip curled. 'What is *that*?'

Chiara glanced down to see Spiro, looking in the general direction of the man and emitting a low growl. She put her hand on his head and looked at her uninvited guest. 'He's my dog and you're upsetting him. This is my home and I'd like you to leave.'

His gaze came back to rest on her and Chiara fought not to fidget under that exacting expression.

'This is precisely what I've come here to discuss—the fact that this home is not actually yours at all.'

Chiara's insides seized. Was this man from the bank? She forced herself to ask, 'What are you talking about?'

He didn't answer right away. Instead he put his hands in his pockets, drawing Chiara's eye to his mid-section. Heat climbed up her neck and face and she diverted her gaze before he might notice. But he didn't notice. He was looking up at the walls and turning around in a small circle.

He said, as if to himself, 'I've waited a long time to be here...'

Then he started walking towards the reception room Chiara had just vacated. She went after him. 'Excuse me, Signor Domenico...'

He turned to face her from the middle of the room and Chiara had the strangest sensation that *she* was the guest—and not a very welcome one.

'It's *Santo* Domenico.'

Chiara bit out the name. 'Signor *Santo* Domenico. I insist you tell me what on earth this is all about or I will call the police.'

Now she was beginning to panic. He *must* be from the bank. But were they allowed to show up like this? Why had the solicitor not warned her this might happen so soon?

Chiara's head was starting to hurt again.

He looked around. 'Where are the staff?'

Chiara felt defensive and wasn't sure why. 'There are no staff—not that it's any business of yours.'

He looked at her, incredulous again. 'How have you kept this place?'

Chiara knew that was also none of his business, but this whole meeting had taken a surreal turn and she found herself saying, 'We closed up the rooms we weren't using and just maintained the few we needed.'

'You and your parents?'

'Yes. They were buried in a double funeral two days ago, in case you weren't aware.' She was hoping to shock him into some kind of realisation that he was here at a very inappropriate time.

He nodded his head. 'I am aware, and I'm sorry for your loss.'

He couldn't have sounded less sorry.

Before Chiara could formulate another word he said, 'You had a meeting with your solicitor the other day?'

'Yes,' Chiara said faintly. 'How did you know?'

'It's customary to have the reading of the will and such after the funeral.'

'Of course.'

She cursed herself for feeling paranoid. She had no reason to feel paranoid. If he wasn't from the bank then he had to be the businessman her solicitor had mentioned. She forced herself to calm down. There would have to be due process before anyone evicted her from her own home.

'So you will now be aware that this *castello* is in danger of being possessed by the bank unless you can drum up the necessary funds.' Here he stopped, and looked around again before saying, 'Forgive me if I'm speaking out of turn, but I don't think that's likely.'

Chiara wanted to point out that he'd been speaking out of turn since the moment he'd materialised on the doorstep, but that wasn't the issue here. 'Are you from the bank?'

He shook his head and a small smile played around that disturbing mouth, as if her question was amusing for some unknown reason. It made her want to slap him when she'd never before felt violent towards anyone in her life.

'So how do you know that information, then?'

He shrugged minutely and looked back at her. 'I have my sources and I've had a…a keen interest in the *castello* for some time now.'

'A keen interest…?' Chiara struggled to make sense of his cryptic response.

He faced her squarely then, and she had the

uncomfortable sensation that he was about to be a lot less cryptic.

'Yes, a keen interest. For my whole life, in fact. Because, you see, the truth of the matter is that this *castello* actually belongs to *me*. To my family, specifically—the Santo Domenicos.'

Nico looked at the woman standing just a few feet away. She couldn't be more nondescript, in a black shapeless dress, with long light brown hair and not a scrap of make-up. His first impression of her had been that she had to be the housekeeper, but now he noticed the proud bearing of her form. Spine straight, shoulders back...

His conscience pricked—her parents had just died. But he quashed the spark of compassion. This day had been coming for decades and now it was finally here.

His father had died a bitterly disappointed man, and countless other members of his family had suffered as a result of this woman's family's actions. He'd suffered too, enduring jeers and taunts his whole life.

'You're not one of the powerful now, Santo Domenico—you're nothing...'

But he wasn't nothing any more. He had sin-glehandedly pulled himself out of the streets of Naples and achieved stunning success, and now he was finally ready to reclaim his family's her-itage from the people who had stolen it so many years ago.

His one regret was that his father hadn't lived to see the *castello* returned. That he hadn't lived to see where his ancestors were buried and pay his respects. His father had come here once, with his own father's ashes, and asked if he could scat-ter them in the family plot, but he'd been turned away like a beggar.

Nico would never forget the humiliation etched into his father's face and the rage burning in his eyes.

He'd said to Nico that day, *'Promise me you'll walk through those gates one day and reclaim our legacy...promise me.'*

And here he was, finally on the verge of fulfill-ing that promise—except much to Nico's frustra-tion he wasn't feeling exactly satisfied. He was distracted by the realisation that Chiara Caruso's eyes were a very light green. And that she wasn't perhaps as plain as he'd first thought. She was...

intriguingly fresh-faced. Untouched. He was used to women covered in so many layers of artifice, or filled with so many chemicals, it was hard to know what they looked like underneath it all.

She shook her head now, frowning. 'What are you talking about? This *castello* can't belong to you. It's belonged to my family for hundreds of years.'

Anger made Nico's voice tight. 'Are you sure about that?'

Suddenly she seemed hesitant. 'Well, of course...'

'Perhaps you're an expert denier of history, like your father was. Are you really expecting me to believe that you aren't aware of what happened?'

She went pale. 'Leave my father out of this. How dare you appear on my doorstep with some fantastical tale?' She stood back and extended her arm towards the door. 'I'd like you to leave now. You are not welcome here.'

For a moment Nico's conscience pricked again, he thought that perhaps he should leave and at least allow her a period of private mourning before returning in a couple of days. But then he registered her words: *you are not welcome here.* Exactly the same words her father had said to *his* father when he'd tried to gain access to the family burial plot.

Nico planted his legs wide. He wasn't going anywhere.

The dog standing beside her emitted another pathetic growl.

He said, 'I'm afraid that it's *you* who is not welcome here. Not for much longer anyway. It's merely a matter of time before the bank moves to take possession.'

Chiara stared at this man who looked as immovable as a stone statue. Against every instinct, her curiosity was aroused. Maybe he wasn't mad—maybe he believed what he was saying.

'What gives you the right to say such things... that the *castello* belongs to you?'

'Because it's true. My family built it in the seventeenth century.'

Chiara wanted to shake her head, as if that might make order out of what he was saying. She'd known the *castello* was old—especially some parts of it—but not that old.

He went on. 'At that time the Santo Domenicos

owned this estate and all the land and villages from here to Syracuse.'

What he was talking about was a huge swathe of land, and if it were true— Chiara shook her head. It couldn't be. 'My family have been the sole owners of this castello for as long as I know—our name is above the door, etched in stone.'

He dismissed that with a curl of his lip. 'Anyone can carve words into a slab of stone. Your family took ownership of this *castello* before the Second World War. The Carusos were the Santo Domenico family's accountants. When we were in financial difficulty they agreed to bail us out, using the *castello* as collateral, the agreement being that as soon as we had the money again we would buy the *castello* back at an agreed price. Then came the war.

'After the war, your family made the most of the chaos at that time. They claimed to have no knowledge of the agreement and destroyed all the paperwork, saying our claims were bogus. So many people were trying to reclaim ownership of land and possessions after the war that the authorities chose to believe that we were being opportunistic. We were a powerful family, and some were only too happy to see us brought down and destroyed.'

He continued.

'The war decimated our savings—we lost everything. We became destitute. Your family refused to negotiate or to give us a chance to regain our property. Our very proud Sicilian family was scattered. Most emigrated to the United States. We ended up in Naples. My grandfather refused to leave Italy, always hoping he'd see our lands returned before he died. As did my father. Both were thwarted.'

Chiara struggled to take this in. 'You *can't* have proof of this. I've never heard mention of the Santo Domenicos in my life.'

He cast her a jaundiced look. 'I don't believe that. Our story is part of local legend around here.'

Chiara flushed when she thought of her very sheltered upbringing. Their housekeeper—before she'd been let go in recent years—had done all the shopping, and her father had gone into the village for supplies since then. Whenever Chiara had ventured out she had noticed the way people looked at her, and she'd burned with self-consciousness because she'd assumed they were judging her less than fashionable clothes and figure.

However, if there *was* any grain of truth to this man's claims, perhaps they'd been judging more than her appearance.

Feeling very exposed, and more vulnerable than ever, she repeated, 'You have no proof of this.'

He arched a brow. 'Come with me.'

He strode out of the room, and Chiara just looked after him stupidly before she kicked into gear. The sensation that he somehow belonged here struck her again and it wasn't welcome.

He walked out of the main door and Chiara had the urge to slam and lock it behind him. But something told her that this man wouldn't be so easily locked out.

He stopped in the main courtyard of the *castello* and looked left and right, as if trying to figure something out, and then strode confidently to the left, towards where the family church and graveyard were situated. The graveyard she'd only walked away from a couple of days ago, after seeing her parents interred.

When she realised where he was headed she hurried to catch up and called out, 'This is ridiculous—you must stop this!'

But he didn't stop. It was as if he couldn't hear her. He got closer and closer to the graveyard, but at the last moment veered away from it and walked to another gate nearby, overgrown with foliage.

She arrived behind him, slightly out of breath. 'What are you looking for? That is the old family plot.'

A place she'd never been into herself, because the housekeeper had used to tell her that it was haunted. A shiver went down Chiara's spine now. Had the housekeeper known something of this man's fantastic claims?

He thrust aside the foliage and located the latch on the gate. At this moment he barely resembled a civilised man. She could see his muscles moving under the material of his suit and felt another disconcerting pulse of awareness in her lower body. Totally inappropriate and unwelcome.

He pushed open the gate and said in a grim tone, 'Come on.'

Chiara had no choice but to follow him into the shadowed and dormant graveyard. Sunlight barely penetrated through the gnarled branches of the trees overhead and it was very still. She picked her way gingerly over the uneven ground, not even sure what she was walking on, hoping it wasn't graves.

He had reached the far corner and was pulling leaves and branches away from something. When she got closer she saw that it was a headstone. He turned to face her with an intense look on his face, and for a moment she was almost blinded by his sheer raw beauty.

Then he took her arm and said impatiently, 'Look.'

Chiara stood beside him, very aware of his hand on her arm and the disparity in their sizes. It took her eyes a moment to adjust, but when they did she could make out faint writing, her heart stuttered and stopped as a dawning dread moved through her.

There, etched in the stone, was the following:

Tomasso Santo Domenico,
born and died at
Castello Santo Domenico,
1830-1897

She couldn't believe it. Castello *Santo Domenico.* Not Castello Caruso.

'He was my great-great-grandfather.'

Chiara looked around, and now she could see the unmistakable shapes of headstones underneath foliage all around her. They seemed to loom at her accusingly in the gloom. The space closed in on her and claustrophobia rose swiftly. She pulled free of Nicolo Santo Domenico's grip and turned and made her way out, her skin clammy with panic.

She almost tripped over a mound, and a small sob came out of her mouth, but then finally reached the gate and stepped into bright comforting sunshine, her head reeling.

Nico stood in the overgrown graveyard, only vaguely aware that Chiara had all but run out of the graveyard. This proof of his family's legacy was almost too much to take in.

Standing in that grand room just a few mo-

ments ago, facing a stricken-looking Chiara Caruso, he'd actually felt a sliver of doubt. Could
this grand, crumbling estate really have belonged to his family? Had they truly once been
the most powerful family in southern Sicily? It
had seemed almost too much to believe when
all he could think of was his grandfather's bitter
countenance and then his father's. Maybe they'd
dreamed it up, frustrated by the struggles they'd
faced. Their fall from grace.

But, no. This graveyard was cold, hard evi-
dence that that they had existed in this place.
That they had once lived, loved and died here.
His ancestors had built it, stone by stone.

A cold sense of satisfaction filled Nico's bones.
He had a right to claim this place now. He was
right to be here.

He knew it wasn't necessarily compassionate to
confront Chiara Caruso just days after her parents' funeral, but he'd never been accused of having compassion.

Faced with this knowledge of how his family
had been left to rot in an overgrown graveyard,
on land that should have been returned to them

decades before, he felt even less inclined to be merciful.

He walked out of the graveyard into the sun, undoing his tie, feeling constricted. Chiara Caruso had disappeared, and yet strangely he found that her stricken expression and those unusual green eyes stayed with him.

He could still feel her arm under his hand. It had been supple and slim, hinting at a more defined body beneath the shapeless clothes. To Nico's shock, the awareness had exploded into more than a frisson, and still hummed in his blood. Disconcerting and not welcome. He put it down to his heightened emotions.

He walked over to the edge of a large uncultivated lawn that rolled down to the sea. There were pine trees along one side and gnarled bushes on the other.

His land.

It beat in his blood now, gathering force. Anger was still high as he thought of his ancestors lying in their cold graves, ignored and left to moulder.

It was one thing to have an intellectual knowledge that something belonged to you, but another thing entirely to experience it. From the moment he'd driven up towards the *castello* he'd felt a sense of ownership that went deeper than the sense of injustice he'd grown up with.

He wasn't usually one to give any credence to intangibles, but right now, for the first time in his life, he felt a sense of *home*. It was as disconcerting as the awareness he felt for Chiara Caruso. It was also something he'd never thought he'd experience after growing up in Naples and being constantly reminded that it wasn't his home.

But as he looked out on this view that the Carusos had stolen from the Santo Domenicos, things didn't feel as clear-cut as they had just a short while before. Nico didn't want to admit it, but Chiara Caruso's reaction to the news had seemed like genuine shock. Either that or she was an undiscovered acting genius.

He'd come here today to present her with a deal she couldn't refuse. A deal that would get him the *castello* within as short a space of time as possible: offering her enough money to sign over the *castello* to him and then go far away, somewhere she, the last of the Carusos, would fade into obscurity.

But that growing awareness of her in his blood

and in his body was blurring the lines and making him hesitate for a moment.

A recent conversation with his solicitor came into his head, a well-worn refrain...

'Nico, you're an outsider, and that has served you well. You've made your fortune by upsetting the status quo and punishing those who've underestimated you. But now it's time to consolidate and expand. It's all very well to be the rogue operator once you have a more respectable life in the background. Right now you're losing out on deals because people feel they can't trust you. You've no family, nothing to lose...'

Nico scowled at the view. He'd been at an exclusive charity event in Manhattan recently, discussing a deal with one of Manhattan's titans of construction. The man's wife had come on to Nico, making her attraction obvious. And, even though Nico had rebuffed her advances, the next day when he'd followed up on a promise to meet and discuss things further, the construction giant had cut off all contact and Nico had lost out on a potentially hugely lucrative deal.

The truth was that he'd had marriage on his mind for some months now. Before his solicitor had even had to say anything it had become evident to Nico that the absence of a wife by his side was damaging his reputation amongst his more conservative peers. And so he'd been facing the unpalatable fact that he should make some adjustments to his very free lifestyle.

To his surprise, the prospect hadn't been totally repugnant. Nico had lived a hedonistic existence for a long time and, to be perfectly frank, he'd been feeling more and more jaded. Tired of the games women played. Tired of the avaricious gleam in their eyes. Tired of not knowing what their agenda was.

While he might once have appreciated the need for a wife who knew how to navigate that world, the thought of a woman like that made something curdle inside him now. As did the idea of growing old amidst the soaring soulless buildings of New York or London.

That might have been where he'd made his fortune, and restored the Santo Domenico pride and name, but standing here on Sicilian land—the land of his ancestors—he knew that the final piece had to be in this place. Nowhere else.

With the evocative scent of the sea and earth

all around him, he found that a new vision was coming to life inside him.

A vision of a future that would help him to achieve the kind of success that he'd only dreamed of up to this point. A vision of a future that included a wife who would give his reputation the sheen of respectability he so badly needed. A wife who would give him a family and breathe the life force back into the Santo Domenico name. A wife who would complement him…who knew the value of legacy.

What he needed was as clear to Nico now as the glittering sea in front of him. It was totally audacious, and contrary to his original plan, but it was taking root inside him and would not be dismissed.

After a few more long minutes Nico turned around to face the *castello*. The only person who had been standing between him and his future— Chiara Caruso—was now the only person who could make sure it happened.

CHAPTER TWO

CHIARA TOOK A sip of the dark golden brandy and winced as it burnt her throat. It was her first time ever taking a drink from the walnut drinks cabinet in the main reception room and she could understand the appeal now, as the alcohol settled in her stomach and radiated a warm, comforting glow.

Her hand still shook, though, and when she heard determined footsteps coming across the stone hall floor beyond the room she put the glass down on a silver tray.

By the time Nicolo Santo Domenico entered the room Chiara's hands were behind her back and she was as composed as she could be, considering she felt as if she'd just been body-slammed by a ton weight.

He stopped in front of her, too close for comfort.

'Well? Is that enough proof for you? A graveyard full of my ancestors?' His voice rang with cold condemnation.

He towered over Chiara and she moved away, across the room, Spiro trotting loyally beside her. She put her hand on the dog's head, as if he could offer protection or a way out of this madness.

Eventually she said truthfully, 'I… I don't know what to say. I had no idea about any of this…'

He lifted a hand. 'Please. I don't know why you insist on this charade of ignorance, because it serves no purpose.' He dropped his hand and his gaze narrowed on her. 'Unless, of course, your parents warned you that this could happen. That once the *castello* was vulnerable again the Santo Domenicos might return to stake our claim…'

Chiara shook her head, feeling sick, wondering just how much her parents *had* known. 'No, they never said anything. I never heard anything.'

He sounded disgusted now. 'That's impossible— unless you were a total recluse.'

Chiara wanted the ground to open up and swallow her whole. His words cut far too close to the bone.

She forced out, 'Whether or not what you say is true…and I have to admit that the graveyard does support your claim…the *castello* is out of your reach as much as mine now. Shouldn't you be talking to the bank instead of me?'

She couldn't stop the bitter note to her voice, still coming to terms with this news herself, so soon after her parents' deaths.

Nicolo Santo Domenico looked at her for such a long moment that Chiara almost snapped at him to stop. She felt like a specimen on a laboratory table, never more aware of her drabness next to his glorious vitality. She would bet that he'd travelled all over the world and probably hadn't been that impressed by it.

And then he said abruptly, 'I presume if you had a choice you would prefer to retain ownership of the *castello*?'

The sharp pang of loss just at the thought of leaving struck Chiara right in her heart. 'Of course. It's my home—the only home I've ever known. My whole family is buried here.'

Like his. Her conscience pricked.

'The only thing standing in your way of retaining the *castello* is a lack of funds.'

Chiara curbed her irritation. 'I'm aware of that,

but unfortunately I don't have the funds.' She had nothing.

'I *do* have the funds.'

Chiara looked at him trying to ascertain where he was going with this. 'Is that why you've come? To humiliate me on behalf of your family by pointing out that you now have the power to buy the *castello*?'

He shook his head, still looking at her with that disconcerting intensity. 'Nothing so petty as that. What I'm saying is that I could give you the funds to pay off the debt and retain the *castello*.'

'Why would you do that?' He didn't strike her as remotely charitable. Certainly not to his family's bitter enemy. He'd been barely civil since he'd arrived.

'I would do that because if *I* was to engage with the bank to buy the *castello* it would be a lengthy and tedious process. The *castello* needs serious refurbishment, and the sooner this happens, the better. I've waited a long time for this opportunity.'

Chiara struggled to try and understand. 'But how do *I* fit into this?'

'Until the bank takes possession you're still

the owner. If you pay off the debt you retain the *castello*. I am offering you a deal to do that on your behalf.'

She looked at him suspiciously. 'Why would I agree to that?'

'Because you'd get to remain at the *castello*. You wouldn't have to leave your home. Isn't that what you want?'

Chiara felt seriously confused now. 'Yes, but… how on earth would that work?'

His dark eyes seemed to bore all the way through her. 'It's very simple, really. You would marry me as soon as possible.'

Chiara looked at Nicolo Santo Domenico in shock. Eventually she managed to formulate words. 'Why on earth would you want me to marry you?'

Apart from anything else, she had to be a million miles removed from the type of woman a man like this went out with. She'd pored over glossy magazines for years, lamenting her untameable hair and full figure. Not to mention her zero fashion sense. She knew her limitations.

'Like I told you, dealing with the bank would be tedious and time-consuming. It would take months—maybe even longer. Through marriage to you the *castello* will become mine within a much shorter space of time.'

Understanding finally sank in. So that was why he wanted to marry her. He was so arrogant and preposterous she could barely take it in. The thought of even considering any kind of intimate relationship with someone like him was totally ludicrous. And yet... She couldn't deny the very illicit beat of awareness deep within her. It shamed her. She wanted his disturbing presence gone.

'I think you've said enough. Your proposal—' She stopped for a second as that word rang in her head. 'It's not even a proposal... What you've just said is frankly ridiculous. I have no desire to marry a complete stranger—for any reason.'

For a moment he looked at her, and then he turned abruptly and went to the window. Much to her disgust, Chiara couldn't stop her gaze moving over his broad shoulders, where the material of his jacket moulded to hard muscles.

He turned back to face her and she lifted her gaze guiltily.

'I should have expected that you would take this as an opportunity to thwart the Santo Domenicos one last time, but you should know that my acquisition of the *castello* is going to happen—with your help or not.'

Chiara felt frustrated. 'I told you—I had no idea about any of this. Why would I want to *thwart* you? What happens to the *castello* once the bank takes possession is out of my control!'

'Not if you marry me.'

He really was serious.

For a moment Chiara let herself imagine what it might be like not to have to leave the place where she'd just buried her parents and a wave of emotion nearly felled her. But at such a cost!

It was all too much.

Chiara felt Spiro nudge her thigh and she went over to sit down in a chair, afraid her legs wouldn't keep holding her up.

She looked up at Nicolo Santo Domenico. 'You can't possibly mean to marry me. You despise me. My family. And why would I agree to such a union? With a man who has married me solely for the *castello*?'

* * *

Faced with Chiara Caruso, back in this room, Nico was more convinced than ever that his plan was a good one. He knew exactly why she should agree to such a union. To give him what he wanted. To repay some of the huge debt her family owed *his* family. What better wife could he choose for himself than a traditional Sicilian woman? And one who was indebted to him.

'You owe me. You are the last Caruso, and I am the last Santo Domenico.'

She stood up, agitated. 'I don't owe you my life!'

'My deceased ancestors lying outside in the graveyard have had *their* lives all but wiped out of history.'

Nico realised that if they married the Caruso name would disappear for ever. It called to the devil inside him. Karma.

Chiara's hands were clasped in front of her and Nico was aware of her breasts, full and high, moving rapidly under her dress. A spike of arousal went straight to his groin and he had to control his response with an effort that was surprising.

He had to admit that this attraction he felt was unprecedented, and had inspired this audacious plan even though she wasn't remotely his type. But something about her lush and curvy body called to a very base part of him that seemed biologically programmed to recognise a mate, regardless of what his head might want.

He'd done some research on Chiara Caruso before this meeting and had found no pictures and little or no information. She didn't appear to have done much at all. Not attended university nor worked.

She was looking at him now with wide, clear green eyes and he felt very warm all of a sudden. It was as if she could see all the way through him and right into his mind. Read his thoughts. It was a very disconcerting sensation for someone who kept his innermost thoughts private.

But it wasn't disconcerting enough to make him change his mind. He'd come to Sicily to reclaim his family's legacy and he vowed right now that he wouldn't be leaving without making this woman his wife. Whatever it took.

He said, 'What I'm proposing is a marriage of convenience. A business transaction. I will put up the money to pay off the bank and in return you will marry me and sign a contract that gives me sole ownership of the *castello*. However, through marriage to me, you will have the right to live here for the rest of your life.'

She went pale. 'Are you totally out of your mind?'

'Not at all. In case I'm not making myself absolutely clear, I don't see this marriage as anything more than a business merger and a way to have heirs. Through them, the Santo Domenico name will flourish again after being all but decimated.'

Heirs? Chiara barely registered that as shock reverberated through her body. 'But me… Why would you want to marry me when you could marry any woman in the world?'

'Like I said, I have no desire to deal with the bank on this matter. And as I never intend to marry for love—'

'Why not?' she interrupted, momentarily distracted enough to want to know if there was some reason for his cold-bloodedness.

Nico's insides clenched. Because his mother had abandoned him and his father when Nico was just weeks old and left his father a bitter, broken man all his life. Because people used love as a way to manipulate and distract. Nico had almost lost everything he'd built up because he'd fancied himself in love with a woman. Thankfully he'd come to his senses just in time. It was a lesson he'd never forgotten.

He looked at Chiara. 'Because I don't believe in it. As for choosing you as my wife… Marriage to you gets me the *castello* and, on a practical level, you have grown up on this estate. You're part of it and you know it. I plan to do extensive renovations, and as I have offices in New York, London and Rome it will help to leave the project in the hands of someone who cares about the estate.'

Chiara shook her head as if to try and clear it. 'You're talking about a project manager, not a wife. How could you propose to bring heirs… *children*…into a loveless marriage like that?'

Something caught his eye behind her and he strode over to a small table and picked up a framed photo of her and her parents. He held it up, his lip curling contemptuously. 'Are you expecting me to believe you were a blissfully happy family?'

Chiara squirmed inwardly. She and her mother

were smiling, but her father had that look of perpetual disappointment on his face.

Hating Nicolo Santo Domenico with a ferocity that shocked her, she went over and took the picture out of his hand, saying, 'We weren't perfectly harmonious, but we were happy in our own way.'

Liar, whispered an inner voice.

Chiara put the picture down and moved out of the man's dangerous proximity.

He said coolly, 'You've just proved my point. There's no such thing as a harmonious family. Surely it's better for children to grow up in an environment where they see their parents working as a team, with mutual respect, rather than something as ephemeral as *love*?'

'But how can you say you'd *respect* me?'

'I personally have no grudge against you, Chiara, in spite of what you may think. My father and every generation before him grew up despising the Carusos for what they did. They were emotional about it and that's why they failed to get anywhere. *My* success came from taking out the emotion.'

He'd cut out emotions long ago. The day he'd found his lover in bed with his best friend.

Nico and his friend had been about to sign a lucrative deal with one of Naples's biggest entrepreneurs, but his girlfriend had believed his friend to be the one instrumental in the deal and so had seduced him in a bid to feather her nest.

She'd begged forgiveness when she'd realised her mistake, but Nico had cut her out of his life and embraced that cold focus ever since.

Chiara Caruso was not the kind of woman who would arouse disturbing emotions or passions. She was perfect.

He said, 'As much as I'm restoring the Santo Domenico name to where it belongs, I'm also proposing this for sound business reasons. This region of Sicily has been woefully neglected and is full of potential. My plans go far beyond this estate. I've already bought all the neighbouring land. I see you as an asset to this estate, Chiara. You'll be invested in it and in its success in a way that no other woman could be.'

Chiara looked at the man and realised the extent of his ruthlessness. Even if she didn't agree to marry him—*and of course she wasn't going to marry him!*—she had no doubt he would do everything he'd just said. Including marrying someone for convenience and heirs. All she represented to him was a means to get to his destination faster.

She stood up. 'I don't understand why it has to be marriage—you could offer me a deal to buy the *castello* before the bank gets involved.'

'That was my plan originally. But since coming here...meeting you...it's changed. Now the stakes are higher, and I'm offering you an opportunity to stay in your home.'

As your chattel, thought Chiara, shocked at the lengths to which he would go, the depth of his need for vengeance.

She refused to let him see how intimidated she was. 'Well, as of this moment, I'm still the owner of the *castello*, Signor Santo Domenico, and quite frankly you're the last man on this earth I'd ever think about marrying.'

He looked completely unperturbed. 'So you're willing to walk away and never see the *castello* again? You strike me as the kind of woman who dreamed of getting married and having a family here.'

Chiara flushed all over. Was her innermost fantasy of dispelling the loneliness of this place with a large and loving family so painfully obvious? But in her fantasy she'd meet the love of her life, go travelling, and then return to the *castello* to live out the life she'd never had here, filling the place with happy sounds and not the echoing silence of her youth.

Feeling exposed, she said tightly, 'You have no idea what kind of woman I am, *signor*. Now, if you've said your piece, please leave.'

Once again Nico's conscience struck when he thought of the freshly dug graves he'd seen in the newer graveyard just a short while before. Perhaps this was evidence of what a life denying your emotions did to you. You became numb to everything except the goal. And the goal was almost in sight.

But something about the shadows under Chiara Caruso's eyes and the way she held herself made him feel uncomfortable. She looked delicate all of a sudden. Very alone in this huge room, with only an ancient dog for company.

Maybe she *was* a recluse?

He ignored the spark of curiosity—she was perfect for what he needed in his life, and that was all that mattered.

He took a business card out of his pocket and held it out. With palpable reluctance she reached out and took it from him. Nico noticed that she had small graceful hands. Unvarnished practical nails. His body stirred against his will, an image of those hands reaching out to touch his naked flesh surprising him with its vividness.

He gritted his jaw. 'Those are all my numbers, including my private one. I'm staying at a villa not far from here till tomorrow lunchtime. You have until then to consider my offer. If I don't receive a call I'll assume you're not interested.'

Chiara's head was bent down over the card as if she was studying it intently. A lock of long hair trailed over one shoulder and it gleamed a light mahogany in the light. His eye was drawn to her waist. Once again he could sense that her clothes were disguising a very classic feminine shape. The kind of shape that had been out of fashion for years but which was proving to be potent enough to snare his interest.

For a moment he hesitated, wondering if he

was crazy to seek commitment with this woman. She intrigued him now, but could she sustain his interest for the length of a marriage? His sexual interest?

If the strength of his attraction was anything to go by, his body was telling him *yes*. And he was reminded of how little had sparked his interest in recent months. Certainly none of the tall, angular women he'd favoured before.

His wife would also be the mother of his children, and Nico surprised himself with a surge of conviction that he wanted a woman who would care for her children and not abandon them as he had been abandoned.

He couldn't trust any woman not to abandon her children, but at least Chiara Caruso knew about legacy—even if it hadn't been rightfully hers. She understood it. And evidently, if the state of the *castello* was any kind of indication, she was a woman who had been deprived of the better things in life. In Nico's experience it wouldn't take much to accustom her to the kind of luxuries he could provide.

But she was refusing to meet his eye now. Nico was used to women gazing at him with naked adoration and a lust that barely masked their instant summing up of his net worth. It was a silent dialogue he knew well and which he welcomed—because there was no game-playing or pretence of emotions that weren't there.

He wasn't used to this…this uninterest. Or antipathy. And he found that, refreshing as it was, it irritated him.

'Chiara.' His voice sounded tight.

Eventually she looked up and he saw fire in the depths of her eyes, making them glow. 'I did not give you leave to call me by my name.'

His pulse throbbed. A sizzle of something deeper than arousal infused his blood. Nico had to admire her spirit. Not many had the confidence to speak back to him and he realised that he'd underestimated her.

He dipped his head slightly. '*Scusami.* Signorina Caruso. I am offering you an opportunity to stay in your family home, which is more than anyone in your family ever did for anyone in mine. Think about it.'

Chiara desperately wanted to look away from those deep-set dark eyes but she couldn't. It was as if his gaze was winding a spell around her, holding her captive. The air vibrated with a kind of electricity between them.

She wanted him gone, so she could try and process everything that had just happened, so she said the only thing she knew that would make him leave. 'Fine. I will consider your offer.'

Nicolo Santo Domenico inclined his head and then he walked out.

Spiro trotted after him, as if to make sure he really was leaving.

Only when Chiara heard the powerful throttle of his car's engine did she move and go back over to the window, catching a flash of silver as it disappeared down the drive. She shivered, as if a cold finger had just danced down her spine.

The first thing Chiara did was to ring her solicitor and ask him for the deeds of the *castello*.

His sharp response—'Why do you want to see them?'—merely heightened the churning in her gut.

She asked him bluntly, 'Is it true that this *castello* once belonged to another family?'

The man was silent for a long moment and then Chiara heard muffled sounds, as if he was instructing someone to close a door.

He asked again, 'Why are you asking for this information now, Signorina Caruso? All you need to know is that the *castello* belongs to you until such time as the bank takes possession.'

'Please tell me the truth.' Her hand was gripping the phone receiver.

He sighed. 'Yes, I believe so—the *castello* did belong to another family, but they lost it around the time of the Second World War. The deeds have been in the Caruso name for decades... I really don't see how this has anything to do with—'

Chiara let the phone drop back into its cradle.

It was true.

When she was small she'd been fascinated by history and she'd used to beg her Papa to tell her stories about the *castello* and who had built it centuries ago. She'd wanted to know all about her ancestors—had they been Arab Moors? Or maybe marauding Greeks? Her father had used to laugh off her questions, telling her that her imagination would get her into trouble one day... She saw now how he'd neatly avoided telling her anything about the history of the *castello*.

Because he hadn't known? Or hadn't he wanted

to admit the truth—that it didn't really belong to them?

Chiara felt the *castello* closing in on her, as if now that she knew, it was silently condemning her.

She walked outside, needing to shake off that uncomfortable feeling, Spiro loyally following at her heels. It was cool in the January sunshine and she drew in deep breaths of air infused with the evocative scents of the earth and sea. She'd often thought that if she could bottle this scent she would wear it for ever. It was *home.*

A home she was about to lose.

She'd spent so long yearning to see the world, but she'd never expected to be thrust out into it so precipitately. She didn't feel ready.

Chiara avoided the area near the small chapel and the graveyard and went down to her private place by the shore. It was a tiny sandy cove, sheltered on all sides by rocks. She sat on the rough sand and pulled her knees up to her chest, wrapping her arms around them. Spiro sank down beside her.

It was only now that she could let the tears flow—for her parents and for the shock of learning just how precarious her position was. She cried for a few minutes, until her face started to feel puffy, and then she forced herself to stop, wiping at her cheeks with the sleeves of her dress. She never usually indulged in self-pity.

She thought of Nicolo Santo Domenico in his bespoke suit, oozing sophistication and success. Arrogance. Retribution. Threat and a kind of redemption all at once. She'd never met anyone so ruthlessly compelling.

Giving in to an urge to find out more about the man who had just blown apart what little security she'd felt she had left, Chiara went back into the *castello* and fired up her father's ancient desktop computer.

Eventually it came to life, and she sat down in a worn leather chair to search for information on the Santo Domenicos.

The first thing to come up were pictures of *him*, looking even more astoundingly handsome than she remembered, dressed in a tuxedo at glittering functions. And in each one there was a stunning woman on his arm. Blondes, brunettes, redheads. He didn't appear to have a preference. They were all tall, slim and intimidatingly beautiful.

He wasn't smiling in any of the pictures. He looked driven. Stern.

Chiara quickly clicked on some other links that told the fabled story of how Nicolo Santo Domenico had displayed his entrepreneurial skills from an early age in Naples. He'd honed those skills and at the tender age of twenty-one had gone to New York and become a millionaire. Within five years he'd become a billionaire and a legend.

She unearthed a very old article from an Italian newspaper, asking what had happened to the once all-powerful Santo Domenico family from Sicily. There was no mention of the *castello*, just a general reference to the fact that they'd once owned huge tracts of land in Sicily but had lost it all. The implication was that perhaps the Santo Domenicos had run foul of the mafia.

Chiara shivered again, absorbing the information. Of course all this didn't mean that Nicolo Santo Domenico would have a leg to stand on if he was to challenge ownership of the *castello* in a court, but the fact was that the bank now owned the *castello*—or as good as. Nicolo Santo Domenico was merely capitalising on the fact that

the *castello* was now available to him in a way
it had never been before.

She stood up and walked slowly through the
castello, noting how many of the rooms had long
been shut up, with their furniture covered in dust-
sheets. Everywhere was crumbling and falling
apart. It had been in disrepair for as long as Chiara could remember. The truth was that they'd
never really been able to afford it—even when
their crops had been providing an income.

The *castello* deserved to have new life breathed
into it. Chiara's heart squeezed to think that she
wouldn't be here to see it. And then she realised
she also wouldn't be here to tend her parents'
grave. Or her grandparents'.

It was unutterably cruel to think of the *castello*
being shut to her when her own family were laid
to rest here.

As Nicolo Santo Domenico's were.

But, reminded a small inner voice, *Nicolo Santo
Domenico is offering you a chance to stay.*

Through marriage.

The thought of marrying a man like him left
her breathless with a number of conflicting emotions.

She'd never in a million years imagined that the faceless man she'd fantasised about all her life would actually appear on her doorstep, but as soon as she'd seen Nicolo Santo Domenico's hard and beautiful features she'd felt a pull of recognition deep inside, as if finally she had a face to put to the handsome prince of her dreams.

She felt disgusted at herself now. At the years of naive dreaming in a home that hadn't even been rightly hers.

And Nicolo Santo Domenico hadn't come for *her*. He'd come for the property, she reminded herself soberly. She was just a convenient by-product. Or a bonus. She shivered again, but this time it was in reaction to imagining what sharing intimacies with Nicolo Santo Domenico would be like.

Chiara saw her reflection in the window. She knew how she looked—plain and boring. Un-varnished. She'd inherited her large breasts from her paternal grandmother, along with her average height and the hourglass shape which had gone out of fashion about fifty years ago.

One day Chiara had heard her father say to

her mother, *'Our daughter won't turn heads, but she'll make some man a fertile wife.'*

Her cheeks burned again as the humiliation came back. And then she crushed the thought. She shouldn't be thinking ill of her father. But he had grown bitter after his wife hadn't been able to have any more children and he'd been denied the son he'd desperately wanted. Chiara wondered now how much of that had had to do with his knowledge of the provenance of the *castello.*

Had he wanted a son to ensure the Caruso name stayed alive within the *castello* because he'd known of the history?

Chiara let herself consider Nicolo Santo Domenico's...*proposition.* Surely he couldn't really mean to marry her? Was he really ruthless enough to convince himself that marriage to an unsophisticated Sicilian woman was worth the price of regaining his family inheritance?

Anger rose inside Chiara at the thought that he could treat her like a pawn. And that he'd assumed to know her, based on what he had judged of her appearance and demeanour. The fact that he hadn't been completely wrong made her pride smart. But there was so much more to her than a mere dream to marry and love in this place.

No matter what he'd said here today, he couldn't truly mean to go through with a marriage to a complete stranger.

Chiara thought of Nicolo Santo Domenico's expression when he'd left—almost smug. As if he'd achieved exactly the outcome he'd expected and knew she'd come around in the end, in spite of her refusal.

She wanted to dent that smugness. She wanted to shock him as he'd shocked her. She wanted to see him look as surprised as she must have looked this afternoon. She wanted to call his bluff and witness his panic when he really thought through the repercussions of his arrogant assumptions and demands.

CHAPTER THREE

NICO DIDN'T LIKE the sense of anticipation he felt as he waited for his driver to return with Chiara Caruso. When she'd rung him earlier that morning he'd offered to meet her at the *castello*, but she'd told him she'd prefer to meet him at his villa, so he'd sent someone to fetch her.

He paced back and forth on the terrace that wrapped around the side of the modern villa with its stunning view of the sparkling sea. From here he could see the land around the *castello* but not the actual building, which was a mix of architectural styles dating all the way back to his early ancestors, who had been Spanish. There were elements of Moorish architecture, and then more classical bits had been added over the years.

The effect was a snapshot of Sicilian history— a potent symbol of longevity and survival which had withstood the ages on its dramatic promontory overlooking the sea.

The emotional punch from his first view of the *castello* and his visit to the graveyard yesterday still lingered. The sense of urgency to reclaim what was his was even stronger now. As was his urge to claim Chiara Caruso. Last night he'd found her image stealing into his brain with a vividness that had unnerved him. He'd told himself it was only due to the fact that he'd decided to include her in his plans. Not because he hungered to know the secrets she hid under her shapeless outfit. Not because base instincts he hadn't indulged since he was a teenager had resurfaced. He was more than that now.

He heard a noise behind him and turned around to see the uniformed housekeeper leading Chiara out to meet him. He settled back against the wall and watched her walk towards him, unconsciously tensing himself against those base instincts she'd ignited so effortlessly within him.

But it was no use. In spite of the fact that she looked as if she belonged to another era, wearing a starchy white shirt with a big collar and a boxy dark jacket, arousal hummed in his blood. It was almost galling. A calf-length skirt did nothing to enhance her figure, and nor did practical flat shoes. Her hair was pulled back from her face and left loose and wavy around her shoulders.

It had been a long time since Nico had had any woman presented to him who wasn't coiffed to within an inch of her life. If he hadn't been so unnerved by the strength of his attraction to her he might have found it refreshing.

She walked out into the sunshine and he saw she was pale. The vivid green of her eyes stood out, unusual and arresting. He fought not to let his gaze drop to the full line of her breasts and straightened up, indicating for her to take a seat at a table nearby set with coffee and tea and small cakes.

She looked at the table, and then back at him. 'I'd prefer to stand.' She held a capacious black bag in front of her like a shield.

He faced her. 'Very well. Have you thought about what I said?'

Chiara could hardly breathe. Nicolo Santo Domenico was—unbelievably—even more gorgeous than she remembered. With his back to the astounding view, dressed in a white shirt with its top button open and sleeves rolled up and dark trousers, he could have stepped directly from the pages of a fashion magazine for men.

The villa was breathtaking too, in its modern simplicity, built into a cliff overlooking the sea. A total contrast to the *castello* and its ancient crumbling history. She'd never seen so much pristine white furniture.

It hurt to look directly at the man, but she forced herself to meet his dark gaze. She'd felt full of bravado yesterday, but right now that was in short supply. Why had she thought it was a good idea to come here? What had she wanted to prove? She couldn't turn back now—he expected her to say something...

And then she remembered. The shock and humiliation. The desire to see him lose some of that cool sense of entitlement.

She took a breath. 'I have thought about what you said, Signor Santo Domenico, and I've decided that I'll accept your offer.'

Chiara's heart was beating so hard she felt lightheaded. She waited for Nicolo Santo Domenico to register what she'd said and then panic. Except he didn't look like a man who would ever panic about anything. He looked supremely assured. Not a flicker of reaction crossed his face. Had he heard her?

She felt panicky. 'I said—'

'I heard you,' he said. 'Are you sure about this?'

Chiara had a sickening sensation that she'd misjudged how to handle this situation badly. She forced herself to nod. 'Yes. I'm sure. I want to marry you.'

'*Va bene.*'

He pushed himself away from the wall and strode back into the villa. Chiara turned to watch him, her panic intensifying. She followed him inside. He picked up a mobile phone and made a call. She heard him speak to someone on the other end.

'We will proceed with drawing up the contracts. Chiara Caruso has consented to be my wife.'

When he'd terminated the conversation he looked at her and frowned.

'What's wrong? You look like you've seen a ghost.'

'I thought… I thought if I said yes that you'd come to your senses.'

His frown grew deeper, and then something

flickered in his eyes. Surprise? 'You called my bluff? You didn't think I really meant it?'

Now Chiara flushed. 'I just thought that when it came to it...to the prospect of taking me as your wife...' She stopped.

He shook his head and walked towards her. 'Oh, no, *cara*, you need to realise that I *never* make empty propositions.'

Chiara saw it then—the steely determination in his eyes. He wanted the *castello* badly enough to marry her. He really was that ruthless.

Feeling desperate, she said, 'But I'm not the kind of woman a man like you marries.'

'You do yourself a disservice, Signorina Caruso.'

His gaze flickered over her and her father's words came back to mock her, *'She'll make some man a fertile wife.'*

She didn't want to be a brood mare! She wanted to be loved passionately. This had been a really stupid idea. She should never have thought she could goad him.

She stepped back. 'I'm sorry. I've changed my mind. I can't do this.'

Chiara had started to walk out of the vast open space when she heard him.

'Signorina Caruso, wait.'

She stopped reluctantly. Nicolo Santo Domenico walked around her to stand in front of her. He looked incredulous.

'You would really prefer to walk away with nothing when I can offer you a life of ease and luxury? I am a very wealthy man, *cara*.'

Chiara didn't need to be reminded of his single-minded pursuit of success. She was watching it in action. 'I know. I looked you up.'

'Well, then, you know I am not making empty promises. I have homes in New York, Rome and London, as well as an island in the Bahamas.'

Chiara's heart squeezed. She'd longed to see those places all her life. But not like this. Not via a marriage of convenience to a cold-hearted vengeful titan of industry. She couldn't even begin to imagine what such a thing would be like. Day to day. Waking up next to a man who seemed far too powerful and dynamic to need something as banal as sleep.

She realised to her horror that she must have

articulated something of her thoughts out loud when he folded his arms and answered her.

'I work mainly at my office in Rome, but I travel frequently to the States and London. You would be expected to accompany me when required, for necessary functions and social events. But in the main I see the *castello* as being my base—which is where you will reside when I don't require you.'

When I don't require you. Like an employee.

His arrogance was astounding. And yet the thought of leaving the *castello* behind for good was excruciating. *This can't be my only option,* she thought a little desperately.

'If I don't agree to marry you, would you allow me access to the *castello*? To visit my parents' and grandparents' graves?' At least if she had access she might not feel as if all links had been be severed.

A hard expression settled over Santo Domenico's features. 'Why would I when your own family didn't ever allow that basic access to us?'

Her insides tightened. Her father had been zealous about privacy and had only let staff or estate workers enter the *castello* grounds. She had a suspicion now that it had been a reflex, handed down from generations, dating back to when they'd had reason to be paranoid about intruders. *The rightful owners.*

'In answer to your question, I would afford you the same respect as was afforded to *my* family—so, no, you would not be granted access. Within a very short space of time, Signorina Caruso, your claim on the *castello* and this place will be gone for ever. It will be as if you never existed.'

Nicolo Santo Domenico's words were horrifyingly stark and brutal. Emotion rose. Terrified he would see it, Chiara whirled around and went back outside to stand at the terrace wall. Her eyes stung and she blinked rapidly.

The view was a view she'd looked out on herself many times, and yet she knew she'd never get tired of it. The scents…the sounds of this place… they were as much a part of her as her own flesh and blood.

She'd actually been born in the *castello*, because her mother had gone into labour three weeks before her due date. The housekeeper had helped her to give birth, but due to complications after the birth, and the delay in getting her to the hospital, her mother had not been able to have more children.

In spite of that, Chiara had always secretly loved the fact that she'd been born within the *castello* walls. As if she was as much a part of its fabric as the stones. She'd often wondered how many babies had been born there.

As much as Chiara had always wanted to travel and see the world, she knew she wouldn't last long unless she could return to this place. It fed her soul. The thought of leaving here and never being able to return was more than she could bear.

Nicolo Santo Domenico would take owner-ship no matter what—she didn't doubt that—and soon there would be fancy electronic gates permanently locking her out from her past and her ancestors. Removing her from the anchor of her life.

Chiara forced herself to try and cut through the emotion to think clearly, and her first thought was a churlish one—she'd only known Nicolo Santo Domenico for less than twenty-four hours and already he had an influence on her.

She'd called his bluff and it hadn't worked. Clearly he was willing to go as far as marriage.

Chiara looked out over the view and realised there was nothing between her and a precipitous drop to the sea except the terrace wall. She felt dizzy for a moment, as if the wall had suddenly disappeared and she was teetering on the edge of a vast void.

The question slid into her mind and she couldn't stop it. *What if you said yes? What if you just said...yes?*

She wouldn't have to take that leap into the void. She wouldn't have to face the heartache of never being able to pay her respects to her parents...her grandparents. She would see the *castello* restored to its former glory. A glory she'd never really witnessed.

Nicolo Santo Domenico might be willing to go as far as marrying her *now*, but once he saw how lacking she was in social graces and worldly sophistication—once he saw how unsuitable she was to be his wife—surely he'd realise that he'd made a huge mistake and call it off, move on to a more suitable woman?

A seed of hope bloomed in Chiara's gut. If they

got divorced wouldn't she then have a chance to negotiate terms for access to the *castello*? At least visitation rights? It wouldn't be lost to her for ever.

For the first time since she'd heard his outrageous proposal, marriage to Nicolo Santo Domenico didn't seem like such a ridiculous suggestion.

Chiara heard a noise behind her and tensed— as much against the noise as at the way her blood leapt and her skin grew hot. It was disconcerting to find herself reacting like this. Disconcerting and galling that her own body could let her down so easily.

'Signorina Caruso?'

Chiara took a deep breath and turned around. She wasn't ready to leave her home. Her life. Not yet. Not until she'd negotiated terms to gain access. It was clear he wouldn't give her an ounce of leeway unless she agreed to marry him. But at least if she could do it on her terms then it might be worth the upheaval.

She looked at Nicolo Santo Domenico and told herself that if he wanted to insist on entering into a legally binding state to further his own interests then she would at least ensure that it would protect hers, too.

She lifted her chin. 'I will agree to marry you— but on one condition.'

There was a long beat of tense silence and then he inclined his head slightly and said, 'Not that you're really in a position to negotiate…but I'm listening.'

Chiara nearly crumbled at the last second, but she knew this was the only way she'd have a chance of keeping any kind of claim on the *castello*.

'My condition is that after six months we review the marriage and see how it's working. And there will be no question of having children until after the six-month trial period.'

As Chiara didn't expect Nicolo Santo Domenico to be remotely interested in giving up the parade of beauties in his life any time soon, she felt fairly confident that in spite of his pronouncement about heirs he hadn't actually planned on having them *now*.

He was silent for a long moment, that dark gaze far too assessing. Chiara fought not to squirm.

Eventually he said, 'That's actually *two* conditions. But very well. I agree.'

Chiara felt light-headed, and her heart palpitated madly as the enormity of what she'd just agreed to sank in, but she told herself she was doing the right thing. The alternative—walking away and never seeing her home again—was unthinkable.

Chiara held out her hand, 'In that case, you may call me Chiara.'

Nicolo Santo Domenico took her hand in his and Chiara almost jumped out of her skin at the electric shock.

He squeezed her hand firmly and said, 'And you may call me Nico. I look forward to getting to know you, Chiara.'

Chiara pulled her hand free abruptly, terrified he might see how he affected her. She knew there was a wall behind her, but suddenly she felt as if she took a step back she would be freefalling over that precipice with nothing to hang on to except the triumphant gleam in Nico's dark eyes.

And it was too late to do anything about it except go forward. And pray that she hadn't grossly underestimated him. *Again.*

* * *

A week later, Chiara's head was still spinning. As soon as she'd made it clear that she would marry Nico, the true extent of his wealth and privilege had become scarily apparent.

There had been a flurry of meetings at the villa with his legal people and her solicitor, who had pulled her aside and wondered if she was quite all right. She'd ascertained that, yes, the bank would take possession of the *castello* as soon as possible, so she'd found out all she needed to know—this was indeed her only option of retaining any contact with her home. Doing a deal with Nicolo Santo Domenico. A devil with the face of an angel and the body of a bare-knuckle fighter. A self-made billionaire who'd lived a life in pursuit of vengeance. Against *her* family.

Contracts had been drawn up and signed, and Chiara's life had been sent spinning in a direction she hadn't ever anticipated.

She looked at herself now, in the mirror of her bedroom at the *castello*. She was wearing the wedding dress that had belonged to her paternal grandmother, whom Chiara had loved dearly. Her *nonna* had shown her the dress before she died and then laid it carefully in its custom-made box, telling Chiara that she would love to think of her wearing it on her wedding day, even though she wouldn't see her.

Chiara had inherited her body shape from her grandmother so the dress fitted almost perfectly. It was a little threadbare in places, but it was still surprisingly pristine. Made of Sicilian lace, it had long sleeves and a high collar. It was demure, and yet Chiara felt very exposed when she noted how it clung almost indecently to her body, showing off her too large bust and hips.

But there was nothing she could do about it now. She was due to go to the *castello* chapel and marry Nicolo Santo Domenico at any moment now.

He had offered to buy her a dress and hire professional stylists, but she'd refused. She'd eventually agreed for him to enlist the help of a couple of local girls, and one of them approached Chiara now with the matching veil for the dress. She'd pulled her hair back in its habitual style and it fell loose and wavy down her back—she'd given up any attempt to tame it.

They attached the veil low on the back of her

head and pulled it over her face, almost obscuring her vision.

Chiara had seen the looks the girls had exchanged as they'd helped her dress, but she didn't care. She knew this wasn't a real wedding, and if her aim was to make Nico regret marrying her as soon as possible then this was the way to go.

They'd barely exchanged two words all week as the preparations had taken over and Chiara had felt ridiculously relieved—even though she knew it was futile to think she could avoid her husband once they were married.

But, thankfully, it looked as if he was as reluctant as she for them to spend any time together. He'd told her as much during one of their brief conversations, saying, 'I will have to return to New York almost immediately to oversee a merger. There won't be time for a honeymoon.'

She'd responded with relief. 'I don't expect a honeymoon—this isn't a real marriage.'

He'd looked at her for a moment, as if he was about to say something else, but then they'd been interrupted and Chiara had taken the opportunity to escape.

Soon, she reassured herself, he would be back in New York, where he would be indelibly reminded of the kind of woman he preferred. By the time he returned to Sicily he would have decided to divorce Chiara and she could negotiate her terms.

She'd already checked with her solicitor and he'd assured her that once they were married, no matter what the contracts said, she would have rights as Nico's wife. That was all she needed to know.

The two girls stepped back. There was a knock on the door and a voice.

'*Signorina*, they are ready.'

Chiara sucked in a breath and tried to quash the ominous feeling that her confidence in predicting the swift demise of this marriage was all too shaky. She'd underestimated Nico before. But this was her only option—unless she wanted to take off the dress, pack it up and walk out of the *castello* for good.

She closed her eyes briefly, sending up a swift plea for a speedy resolution to all of this, and then she opened them again and turned around to face her destiny.

* * *

Nico was surprised at how on edge he felt as he waited for Chiara to appear at the entrance to the *castello* chapel. There was only a handful of guests. Her solicitor and his own legal team. There was no great pretence that this was anything other than a marriage of convenience.

Chiara had been surprisingly co-operative once she'd agreed to marry him, signing every contract put under her nose after brief consultation with her solicitor. In fact she'd been so amenable, particularly about the clauses that dictated how much of his fortune she'd receive if they ever divorced—she'd barely even looked at that part—that he'd had to instruct his own team to go through them again with a fine-tooth comb in case they'd missed something.

He'd given in to her demand of a six-month trial period, but he was confident enough to presume that by the time six months had passed she would be reluctant to give up her new lavish lifestyle.

But a small, annoying inner voice reminded Nico that Chiara had turned down all his offers for clothes, a dress...stylists. How ironic, he thought now, to have apparently found the one woman in the world who truly appeared to have no designs on his wealth—a member of the very family that had stolen his birthright!

There was a movement at the doorway and he narrowed his gaze. When she appeared, though, he wasn't prepared for the punch to his solar plexus. She should have looked ridiculous in the old-fashioned wedding dress, so traditional that it must have been made in the last century. And yet its sheer simplicity robbed Nico of any coherent thought for a moment as Chiara started to walk down the aisle.

Unaccompanied.

And if there was something about that lonely image that sparked some answering echo inside Nico, he denied it immediately.

Quite frankly, he was too distracted by the way the dress effortlessly showcased the full extent of Chiara's curves. The Venus de Milo made flesh. He even saw one of his legal team's eyes widen at the sight of her, and felt a rush of something very hot and possessive. *Crazy.*

If Nico hadn't been so acutely aware of what he was doing and where he was, he might have imagined himself to have slipped back in time some hundred years.

An ornate lace veil framed her face and dark hair. There was a small bouquet of flowers in her hands. When she finally reached his side he caught the delicate scent of wild flowers and earth...the sea. It was evocative and surprisingly sensual.

He turned to face the altar and was reminded again of how petite she was next to him. She reached his shoulder at the most. The priest started to speak, but the words washed over Nico as he realised that he had to restrain himself from reaching out to pull the veil up to see her face.

'I now pronounce you husband and wife. You may kiss your bride.'

Nico turned to face Chiara, overcome with a sense of anticipation he never would have expected to feel for his convenient bride, no matter how much she might stir his blood.

Her head was down-bent and he reached for the veil, pulling it up and over her head. He willed her to look up at him and finally she did. He sucked in a breath. No make-up. Just clear fresh skin and those remarkable eyes. Long dark lashes. And her mouth… Had it always been so full?

He'd never have expected it, but right now all he could think about was how much he wanted to kiss his bride. He caught her chin between his fingers and thumb, angling her face up to his. The church, priest and witnesses were forgotten as he fixated on that lush mouth. As lush as the rest of her, it trembled slightly, and he saw the tiniest hint of a pink tongue. A wave of need rushed through him.

His mouth was on hers before he could stop himself and this was no chaste kiss, mindful of where they were. This was fuelled by unexpected lust and desire. He gathered her to him, feeling those abundant curves press against his body. Soft where he was hard and aching.

It took a long second for him to realise that his brand-new wife wasn't responding as he'd intended. She was like a taut bow against him, quivering but not acquiescing. Her mouth trembled under his but didn't open.

With the utmost reluctance he pulled back and saw those wide green eyes as startled as a fawn's.

Her cheeks were flushed. Her breasts moved rapidly against his chest.

He trailed his thumb down and along her delicate jawline, touched the corner of her mouth, making it open slightly. Right now there was nothing else in the world but this.

Nico said roughly, *'Baciami.'*

Kiss me.

Chiara's whole body was on fire. She was pressed so tightly against Nico's body that she could feel the delineation of every hard muscle under his suit.

This wasn't how it was meant to be! She'd been expecting a peck on the cheek. Nothing more. Then leaving the chapel. Enduring a couple of hours of their pseudo-happy wedding breakfast with total strangers before Nico left in his private jet to get on with his life and his work. Leaving Chiara at the *castello*, to come to terms with her new situation and the hope that she'd be served with divorce papers as soon as possible.

But she couldn't think about any of that now. All she could think of was Nico's firm mouth and how it had felt on hers. Like a brand. A hot brand of ownership. As if he didn't already own her, thanks to the price he'd paid. As if he had to kiss her like that to really stamp his mark on her.

He was still holding her and saying *'Kiss me.'* As if she hadn't just—

His mouth touched hers again, chasing away all coherent thought. And if she'd thought that last kiss was a brand then this was a brutal awakening.

Nico's mouth moved over hers, insistent, masterful. She had no choice but to open up to him, and when his tongue touched hers she almost lost the power of her legs, her insides turning to hot liquid jelly.

She'd longed her whole life to know the power of a transformative kiss. But this didn't feel transformative—it felt cataclysmic. Earth-shattering. Nothing so banal as merely transformative. This was scorching along her insides and lighting a fire deep within her that begged for *more*.

When he finally lifted his head again Chiara was aware of a vague sound and realised it was the priest, clearing his throat with increasing vigour. She felt undone...turned inside out.

She looked up into her husband's dark eyes

and realised she hadn't a clue who this man truly was. And yet she'd just allowed him to breach defences she hadn't even been aware she'd erected over all the years of her isolation here at the *castello*.

She pulled back so abruptly she almost fell, and only Nico catching her arm stopped her. She glared at him, not even sure why she felt so angry. He'd just kissed her. So why did it feel like more than a kiss?

He held her arm and they walked back down the aisle. Chiara's face was flaming. When they stepped out into the bright morning sunshine she was momentarily blinded, but she rounded on Nico anyway, pulling her arm free of his grip.

She opened her mouth, about to demand to know why he'd kissed her like that, but then their guests walked out behind them and she had to close her mouth again. It felt swollen.

Nico led the way back to the *castello*, where he'd hired a local catering company to set up a wedding breakfast.

There she endured the further humiliation of making small-talk with one of Nico's legal team, aware every second that everyone knew this was just a business agreement.

Finally, when everyone had gone—including the caterers—Chiara pulled the veil off her aching head and massaged it with her fingers. She walked downstairs into the kitchen, Spiro at her heels, and for a moment felt grateful that at least she hadn't been separated from him.

After she'd fed Spiro she went back upstairs, wondering if Nico might have already left for New York. But when she walked into the drawing room, he was there, looking moodily at a family photograph of Chiara and her parents, holding a crystal glass in his hand.

She was very aware of the jump in her pulse, reminding her of that kiss and also of that secret part of her which didn't necessarily want to see the back of him so quickly. She was very aware that he'd divested himself of his jacket and waistcoat and she could now see that he wore a close-fitting shirt that left little to the imagination.

Once again she had the realisation that, even though she knew superficial facts about him, she didn't really know him at all.

He turned and saw her, where she stood in the

doorway. He put out a hand. 'Welcome, *mia moglie*, would you like a drink?'

My wife.

The *castello* was now his. *She* was now his. The only thing protecting Chiara from being thrown out on her ear was the fact that she'd married him.

Panic mounted inside her as she questioned if she'd done the right thing. But she'd had no choice! she assured herself, trying to quell that panic.

'Yes, I'd like a drink.'

She walked into the room, trying to appear as nonchalant as possible, as if it was every day that she wore a vintage lace wedding dress that felt glued to her body like an indecent wrap. She'd caught his eyes on her at various times during the day and had wanted to squirm with embarrassment. No doubt he'd been sending up thanks that their wedding wasn't more public. *His unfashionable bride.*

He uncorked a bottle of champagne that had been chilling in a bucket and presented her with a glass of the sparkling golden liquid. She took it from him just as a fresh rush of humiliation landed in her belly as she recalled the kiss they'd shared. She had a suspicion that he'd been toying with her in some way.

She clutched the glass tightly. 'Why did you have to kiss me like that in the chapel, in front of everyone? The only person who doesn't know the truth of this marriage is the priest.'

He looked at her steadily. 'Maybe because I wanted to.'

She stared at him as something indefinable zinged between them. Not possible. Her and him. No way.

'You really didn't need to pretend to fancy me. We both know the kind of woman you prefer.'

He put a hand in his pocket. He couldn't have looked more louche. 'Oh, really? And what kind of woman would that be?'

Chiara's face grew hot. She took a quick sip of her drink, regretting opening her mouth. She tried not to cough as the bubbles fizzed in her mouth and down her throat. When she risked looking at Nico again he raised a brow, still waiting for her answer.

She paced away from him towards the window. Dusk was claiming the sky. How had the day slipped by so quickly? Why was he still here?

She turned around to find an arrested expression on Nico's face and she wrapped her arm around her middle in a subconsciously protective gesture. 'I've seen pictures of the women you like—tall, willowy. Beautiful.'

His dark gaze rose to meet hers. 'I might have agreed with you—until you appeared today looking like the most innocent temptress ever created.'

Reaction set into Chiara's bones and she started to tremble slightly. Nico put down his glass on a side table and moved towards her across the room. He looked as if a civilised layer had been stripped back from his urbane surface and Chiara found it more mesmerising than she wanted to admit.

The air between them crackled. The room suddenly felt sweltering. She might almost have sworn that a fire burned in the massive fireplace just feet away, but a fire hadn't been lit there since Christmas.

He stopped in front of her. She couldn't seem to form a coherent thought. 'I don't… Why are you still here? You were supposed to be getting on a plane to New York.'

He frowned. 'This is our wedding night—why would I be getting on a plane?''

Chiara's head started to throb. 'But it's not a normal wedding.'

He stepped closer. 'This was the perfect wedding. No false declarations of love, no heightened emotions. Just two people coming together for a mutually beneficial cause. To save the *castello.*'

'Which you would have done in any case.'

He shook his head. 'I'm not a patient man, Chiara. I wasn't prepared to wait to regain my inheritance.'

'An inheritance you had to *pay* for.'

It seemed to be important to goad him right now, to keep him back—because she was very afraid that if he came any closer he'd see just how brittle she felt right now. How ready she was to shatter into a million pieces if he touched her again.

This was where her real vulnerability lay. In this space between them that shouldn't exist. Because he shouldn't be looking at her as if he wanted to…to devour her.

He shrugged one wide shoulder. 'The money I couldn't care less about. The *castello* is mine now, and that's all that matters. And into the bargain I have you as my wife.'

'But you don't want me...not like that. You should go...your business must need you.'

If Chiara could just get him to leave now, he'd go to New York and realise that whatever he was feeling for his convenient Sicilian bride was a total aberration. He was a highly sexed man—it oozed from his every pore. He needed to be reminded that she wasn't his type.

But Nico looked straight into her eyes and said, 'On the contrary, I find that I *do* want my wife. Very much.'

CHAPTER FOUR

'ON THE CONTRARY, *I* do *want my wife. Very much.*'

Chiara could barely breathe through the palpitations of her heart. Nico's gaze left hers and moved down. He reached out and took a tendril of her hair that trailed over her shoulder. He twined it around his fingers and tugged gently, so that she had to move forward.

She could feel the heat of his hand through the delicate material of the dress. Her nipples peaked into two hard points and she bit her lip, praying he wouldn't look down.

He said, almost musingly, 'It's been a long time since I saw a woman with hair as long as yours.'

Chiara answered quickly, 'It's not fashionable. I should get it cut.'

He speared her with a dark look. 'Do *not* get it cut.'

Her heart palpitated at his authoritative tone. 'You can't order me not to cut my own hair.'

Nico gritted his jaw for a second, as if biting something back, and then he said with faux politeness, '*Please* do not cut your hair. I like it.'

Chiara knew she was fighting a losing battle. To have all this man's attention focused on her... she'd have to be made of stone not to react.

She was melting into a puddle of lust. Her body felt painfully alive and sensitised. She ached in secret places—between her legs. Her wedding dress suddenly felt constricting, and all she wanted was to feel a cool breeze on her bare flesh. She imagined Nico's big hands reaching for her, pulling the dress apart...baring her to his dark, hungry gaze.

That lurid thought was like a bucket of cold water landing on Chiara's head. *What was wrong with her?*

She jerked away from Nico so fast that her hair pulled and she winced. She realised she was still holding her glass with a death grip and put it down on a nearby table.

She sucked in a breath. Nico looked unperturbed. She gestured between them. 'I don't know what this is... I barely even know you.'

'And yet we're married.'

She glared at him. 'Only because you made sure I was between a rock and a hard place.'

His mouth tipped up slightly and he drawled, 'Believe me, *cara*, I know how *hard* it feels.'

She couldn't stop her gaze from dropping and she saw the bulge pressing against his trousers. She glared at him again, even as her body quivered in reaction to this evidence of his arousal. 'That is disgusting.'

'That is chemistry—and we have it, whether you like to admit it or not.'

Desperation mounted. 'We don't! It's only because you're highly sexed and you probably haven't slept with a woman since you arrived here and—'

He held up a hand. 'Stop. I have been with enough women to know that true chemistry is a rare thing. I haven't wanted a woman this much since—' He stopped at that, his face darkening. 'That's not important. What *is* important is that I want my wife, as unexpected as that fact might be, and I have every intention of consummating this marriage tonight.'

In spite of her instincts, which were screaming at her not to let this happen, for reasons she wasn't even sure she fully comprehended Chiara was intrigued. She wanted to know more about the other woman he'd wanted as much. She wasn't as intrigued by the dart of dark emotion that thought engendered. This man shouldn't be provoking her emotions.

'You're little more than a stranger!'

'And yet I'd say we know more truth about each other than most couples who get fogged up by emotions that aren't real.'

He closed the space between them and Chiara's already weak resistance got even weaker. She'd never experienced such a compelling pull towards another human being. And she hated herself that it was for someone who was so singularly ruthless. That it was for someone who saw her only as a pawn.

He reached for her, placing his hands on her waist and tugging her towards him. She put up her hands, but all that did was bring them into contact with his chest—a wall of hard muscle.

God help her, but she felt it in her bones. The inevitability of what was to come. Because she *wanted* it. Though every self-preserving instinct was screaming at her to run, there was also something rebellious within her stirring to life after all these years, willing her to do the most audacious thing she'd ever done...

Maybe they *did* know more about each other because of the lack of emotion? But in spite of that she desperately needed to know that there was more driving his ruthlessness than just a need to succeed where others had failed.

'Why was it so important to you?' she blurted out.

He frowned. 'Why was *what* so important?'

'The *castello*—getting it back. You said yourself that you felt more detached about it than your ancestors and that's why you were successful. So would it have really mattered if you hadn't got it in the end?'

He tensed, his hands tightening on her waist. 'Why are you asking me this now? It's done.'

'Because I just...need to know.'

His eyes bored into hers. 'I did it for my father, who wanted it for his father, who had memories of this place. It was his dying wish that I return this land to our name and I will always regret that I wasn't able to do it in time. I grew up in Naples, but it was never home. We were reminded of that by the gangs who ran our neighbourhood. We were never welcome. I've never felt at home anywhere. You'll probably think this sounds ridiculous, but as soon as I walked into the *castello* it felt like home...'

Chiara's chest felt tight. She recalled having that impression when he'd arrived—as if he belonged here more than she did. She understood the concept of *home* all too well. She'd been lucky enough never to question hers. Until now. And she knew what grief felt like and had an insight into what it must have been like to want to fulfil a parent's dying wish.

She had a sense that Nico was already regretting saying what he had. She could see his expression closing, becoming impenetrable. Acting on instinct, she put her hand up to his face, tracing his hard jaw.

'I'm sorry your father died before he could come back here.' Her voice was husky. For the first time since she'd met him she felt a moment of affinity with him.

The tension she'd been holding on to eased inside her. Nicolo Santo Domenico wasn't as cool and impenetrable as he appeared.

His hands were still tight on her waist. 'I don't want to talk about that. In fact I don't want to talk at all. I want you, Chiara.'

I want you.

The words sent a thrill of excitement through Chiara. In spite of the fact that everything about this whole situation was unorthodox, and had morphed out of all sense of control, she knew she didn't want to be anywhere else right now.

Trembling from head to foot at the strength of the feelings and desires building within her, she said, 'I want you too.'

Nico's eyes flashed. He pulled her to him, spearing a hand into her hair at the back of her head and curving his other arm around her waist.

When his mouth met hers Chiara almost combusted on the spot. Her fingers clutched at his shirt. She could feel his arousal digging into her belly and it made her ache even harder. The kiss was wild and hot, too consuming for Chiara to wonder if she was doing it right or wonder what Nico would do when he discovered his very traditional Sicilian wife was a virgin.

She had no time to think at all, because Nico broke off the kiss and swept her up into his arms, striding out of the room and up the stairs. He stopped in the corridor and she felt the tension in his bunched muscles.

'Which way?'

Chiara's old bedroom lay to the right, but the master bedroom, which she'd prepared while fully expecting it not to be used, lay further down to the left. She lifted a hand and pointed in that direction and Nico moved, all coiled power and intent.

He strode through the door, kicking it shut behind him. The moon was rising outside, bathing the room in a silvery glow. Nico let her down beside the bed. Her shoes had fallen off somewhere along the way, unnoticed.

She looked up at him, breathless with desire and a kind of wonder that this was actually happening. To someone like *her*. Who had harboured fantasies like this all her life. But the feelings fluttering inside her were too dangerous to try and analyse now—because how could she be feeling anything for someone she hardly knew?

For a taut moment neither one moved, and a sudden cold dread moved through Chiara at the thought that Nico was coming to his senses and wondering what on earth he was doing.

It was the very thing she'd wished would happen. But then he said, 'Turn around.'

Chiara turned around, and the relief rushing through her was more than immense. It was dangerous. Because she knew she should let Nico know just how innocent she was. But she was afraid he'd stop looking at her as if she was the only woman in the world. She wasn't ready for this moment to end. And so she said nothing.

Nico brought his hands up to move Chiara's long hair over one shoulder. He noticed they were shaking. *Dio.* What was wrong with him? He was behaving like a virginal groom who had never undressed a woman before. But he couldn't remember the last time he'd been so hard and aching. He scowled at himself. *Not even then.*

Her hair was heavy and silky. He pulled out the tie holding it back from her face and pushed it aside over her shoulder, to reveal the bare back of her neck. He had an urge to press his lips against that spot and so he did, noticing that her petite frame shuddered slightly.

Who would have known it? he marvelled. That he would have considered marriage to a woman like this and that he would want his convenient wife so much? When he'd first thought it through he'd fully intended for this to be a traditional marriage in all aspects, but even he had considered giving her some space before making this a marriage in bed.

But from the moment he'd watched her walk down the aisle earlier he had known there was only way this day was ending. In this bedroom. *Right now.*

He found the top of her dress and the long line of buttons that ran down her spine. A bead of sweat broke out on Nico's brow, as he painstakingly undid every button until the last one, just above her buttocks. It was a surprisingly erotic experience when he was used to women leaving little to the imagination. The dress gaped open to reveal her pale back and the clasp of her bra.

He undid that and felt her go very still. Giving in to an uncharacteristic moment of conscience, Nico put his hands on her shoulders and asked, 'Okay?'

The fleeting thought occurred to him that

maybe she was innocent, but he dismissed it. In this day and age? No matter how sheltered someone might be, it was nigh on impossible to hang on to any kind of innocence or purity.

He was surprised at how that thought made him feel. Almost disappointed...

She nodded her head and he heard a faint, 'Yes, I'm fine.'

Nico slipped his fingers under the dress and pushed it over each smooth shoulder and down her arms. Now she was bare from the waist up, her back a sinuous curve that made his blood sizzle.

His voice was unbearably rough. 'Turn around, Chiara.'

She waited an infinitesimal moment—enough to have Nico's nerves screaming with tension and need. He almost laughed at the notion that she was innocent now. This women was a siren and she knew exactly what she was doing! She had to! He was on fire.

Chiara's heart was beating so fast she felt light-headed. No one had ever seen her naked before. She'd never even inspected herself in the mirror, shying away from looking at her too pronounced curves.

And yet something new and bold within her compelled her to turn, and when she did an intense heat flooded her whole system. Nico's eyes widened and colour slashed across his high cheekbones. His chest moved rapidly, as if he'd been running.

Chiara's bare breasts felt full and heavy. Nipples tight and stinging. Nico reached out a hand and cupped one full weight in his hand and little beads of sweat broke out on Chiara's brow.

He shook his head, as if dazed. 'I want to see *all* of you.'

Chiara put her hands to the dress, where it hung precariously on her hips, and pushed so that it fell down. Now she wore just her panties.

Nico's hand dropped to his side and Chiara saw him curl both hands into fists, as if to stop himself from reaching out again.

He said, 'I never thought a woman like you could exist.'

Intense self-consciousness flooded Chiara and she brought her arms up to cover her chest and between her legs. 'I'm too big—'

Immediately he stepped forward and took them down, saying, '*No*. You are beautiful. You embody pure sensuality, Chiara.'

She kept her gaze lowered, feeling even more self-conscious now—because she was practically naked while he was still fully clothed.

As if reading her mind, Nico took his hands from her again and started to undo the buttons on his shirt. Now it was her turn to look as bit by bit his chest was revealed, broad and powerful, with a smattering of dark hair that led in a line down his flat muscled abdomen and underneath his belt.

His hands were there now, and he undid his belt and trousers. With an economy of movement he pushed them down, taking his underwear with them. She sucked in a breath, taking in the majestic power of his aroused body, rising proudly from the dark curling hair between his legs. Her mouth watered and she wanted to taste him. It shocked her how carnal she felt. And, how right it felt.

'Chiara...don't look at me like that.'

She looked up, her face burning. He smiled and

there was a falling sensation in her tummy—he'd never really smiled at her before.

'I won't last if you look at me like that.'

Oh.

He took her hand to lead her to the bed behind them and she stepped out of the dress which had pooled on the ground in a mound of silk and lace.

She desperately resisted the urge to believe this moment was special, but it felt significant. She was about to give herself unhesitatingly to a man who had swept into her life and turned it upside down in the space of a week. A man who had behaved in an unbearably ruthless manner but who had shown her that there was something running deep under the surface.

There was more to Nicolo Santo Domenico—Chiara knew it.

He laid her down on the bed and looked at her for a long moment. Then he came down beside her. She desperately wanted to explore his body but she didn't have the nerve. Any anyway he robbed her brain of any power to think when he started to touch her, saying, 'I want to explore every bit of you, taste you...'

He encouraged her to lie back and do nothing

as he proceeded to do just that. He started with her mouth, drugging her with deep kisses, while his hand explored her breast and pinched her nipple, making her turn to liquid and squirm against him, silently pleading for more.

Then he moved down, taking his time, teasing her until her nerves were screaming and she was begging for mercy. When he finally surrounded her nipple with his mouth and sucked it into the hot wet cavern she screamed.

His hand moved down, over her belly and to the juncture between her legs. He pushed them apart with gentle force and Chiara held her breath. He lifted his head and watched her as his fingers explored the place where she ached the most.

She turned away, embarrassed at how turned-on she was, but Nico turned her back to face him as his fingers explored all the way into the heart of her, where she was hot and wet.

'You are so ready for me… It's incredibly sexy, *cara*. And it's the same for me.'

He took her hand and wrapped it around him, exactly as she'd wanted to do herself before. She was awed by the feel of him, steely strong and covered with hot silky skin. He felt so vulnerable and yet never more powerful.

'I need you *now.*'

She looked at him and the moonlight glazed his features with a silvery hue. His expression was stark. She nodded her head and he moved over her body, pushing her legs further apart with his thighs.

She could feel him press against her and had an urge to push her hips up, instinctively seeking that deeper union. He huffed out what sounded like a tortured chuckle, and once again she was struck by this lighter version of Nicolo Santo Domenico and how he made her heart swell dangerously.

He put a hand under her buttocks, angling her up towards him. She was totally at his mercy, and yet she had never felt more powerful than right at this moment. She trusted him implicitly. It came from deep inside her.

And then, with a surge of his body against hers, he thrust deep inside her. Her body bowed in shock and awe at the intrusion. There was a moment of red-hot pain and tears stung her eyes.

He stopped and looked down, the shock she felt mirrored on his face, '*Chiara?* You're a...*virgin*?'

She nodded miserably, all her self-confidence draining away. She fully expected Nico to pull back, disengage, look at her with disgust. But he didn't. Instead something ferocious lit up his expression and he put a hand between them, his fingers touching the point where their bodies met.

'Bear with me, *cara*, it won't hurt for much longer. Trust me.'

She held her breath as Nico started to move again, slowly this time. His fingers moved against her, making her feel something besides pain and discomfort—a burgeoning pleasure.

And then, miraculously, the pain diminished and the glide of his body in and out of hers took on an ease that hadn't been there before. She could feel her body adapting to his and a whole new set of sensations took over. Aligning them. Making her seek a deeper connection.

Instinct took over. This was an age-old dance and Chiara found herself succumbing to its rhythm. She wrapped her legs around Nico's hips and felt him slide deeper. She silently urged him to go harder, faster, as tension mounted in her body and begged for release.

He was remorseless, though, refusing to give in to her demands, eking out her pleasure, until Chiara had to bite into his shoulder to stop herself begging out loud.

And then something snapped inside him…some control he'd been clinging on to—*for her benefit?* The thought was too fleeting to hang on to because Chiara got a sense of how restrained he'd been when his movements became wilder and less controlled, pushing her higher and higher. Finally she climbed to the top of the peak and her whole body tautened like a bow against his for a long, infinitesimal moment, until finally she fell over the edge and into a sea of pleasure more exquisite than she'd ever known, so exquisite that she never wanted it to stop.

Nico's huge body went still and she felt the rush of his release deep inside her—she was too stunned to consider what that meant. He sank over her, deep shudders racking his body, and she could feel her own body still pulsating, milking every last ounce of pleasure from him.

* * *

Nico stood under the pounding shower spray as dawn spread across the sky outside the bathroom window. His body felt wrung out. Weakened from an overload of pleasure.

He braced his hands on the wall, bending his head against the sluicing water as if it might wash away the memory of how completely he'd lost it.

She'd been a virgin. *A virgin.* Nico had never made love to a virgin before—not even when he'd been one himself.

And, to Nico's disgust, his first reaction had been one of very carnal male satisfaction. To know that he was the only man she'd known intimately. To be the first man to wring that unbelievably sensual response from her lush body. To be the first to see her orgasm and feel the contraction of those tight muscles around his—

Dio. He cursed again.

He could still see the look of wonderment on her face after they'd made love. It had taken him completely unawares. He was used to women feigning emotion, not really feeling it. It had to have been because she was innocent. She wasn't like his other lovers. World-weary and jaded. Cynical.

Never in a million years had he imagined that the attraction he felt for Chiara would be so all-consuming and intense. To the point where he hadn't even thought of protection. Something he'd never failed to do with any other lover.

But she's your wife.

That might be so, Nico thought grimly, and he had fully intended theirs to be a marriage that would produce heirs. It was part of his plan. He'd told her that. But he'd also promised to honour the six-month trial period. Even he had thought that wasn't such a bad idea.

But any kind of coherent rational thinking had gone up in flames as soon as he'd seen her naked body.

He tried to curtail the resurgence of desire just from thinking of her. He reassured himself that it was highly unlikely that one night would have got Chiara pregnant. And next time he wouldn't forget.

Next time.

His body reacted forcibly to the thought of introducing his very innocent Sicilian wife to all the pleasures lovemaking had to offer and he cursed through gritted teeth as a slew of X-rated images flooded his brain.

He switched the water to cold.

When Chiara woke it was bright. She could feel a soft cool breeze skating over her skin. The window must be open. She felt incredibly...at peace. Sated in a way she'd never felt before. Even though when she moved experimentally her body ached all over. But not with pain. With remembered pleasure.

And then it all came rushing back—every Technicolor moment of her awakening. She looked round but she knew she was alone in the bed. The sheets were creased. She saw her wedding dress draped carefully over a chair. Nico must have done that, because *she* certainly hadn't given it a thought last night. All too eager to strip off.

She pulled the sheet over her face for a moment, groaning softly. Who had she been last night? A total wanton. A sensualist in training. No inhibitions—or too few to mention.

After that first time Nico had only had to touch her for her to be eager to experience that extreme pleasure again. She had a vivid memory of him moving down her body, pushing her legs apart and putting his mouth on her *there*.

She pulled the sheet down from her face and blinked, trying to will away the rush of heat sweeping up through her body, which was still tender. And yet she knew if he was here right now, looking at her and touching her, she'd probably give in all over again.

Where was he?

She sat up, the sheet falling away from her body. She looked down and could see marks on her breasts. Faint and pink. Evidence of his touch. Mortified, Chiara scrambled from the bed and found a robe to pull on. She belted it tightly and made her way downstairs.

Spiro appeared at the bottom of the stairs, tail wagging. She patted him on the head. There was no sign of Nico in the main rooms or in her father's old office, which she presumed he would take over.

She found him in the massive kitchen. He was dressed in dark trousers and a light shirt, and he was drinking coffee and reading something on a tablet. Chiara felt a rush of self-consciousness as she stood in the doorway.

He glanced up and saw her, and indicated with his head towards the stove. 'I made fresh coffee.' He looked back down at his tablet again. 'The first thing we'll have to take care of here is the WiFi—it's ridiculously slow. And then we need to hire staff. A housekeeper and a maintenance person to start with.'

A lead weight sank into Chiara's belly. She'd had no idea what to expect the morning after a night such as she'd just experienced, but it wasn't this: Nico speaking to her as if she was some kind of assistant, not the woman he'd made love to all night with an ardour that had made her feel—

She slammed a lid down on that thought, terrified that it might show on her face. She shouldn't be feeling anything.

But you are, whispered a little voice.

Chiara walked into the kitchen, acutely aware of her naked body under the robe while Nico was fully dressed. She needn't have worried, though, because he wasn't looking at her. She poured herself some coffee and brought it over to the table, sitting down at the opposite end to her husband.

He was pristine and cool. A million miles from

the passionate lover of last night. He looked up at her and finally something seemed to register.

He put down the tablet. 'How are you this morning?'

Solicitous. Impersonal.

Chiara struggled to keep her frayed emotions in check and to be as cool as him. 'I'm fine, thank you.'

'Bene.' Nico stood up. 'I've made a change in my plans. I'm going to go to Rome today for some meetings and I'll go to New York next week instead.'

Chiara put down the cup, a tiny spurt of excitement making her pulse jump. 'Will I be coming with you?'

He frowned. 'Why would you come with me for business? No, you'll stay here unless there's a social function that requires your attendance. There will be enough for you to do, preparing the *castello* for its refurbishment.'

The spurt of excitement sputtered, but a tiny flickering flame of hope refused to die. She said, 'I thought…after last night…that perhaps our marriage might not be so…businesslike.'

Nico's face was unreadable. 'You were a virgin,

cara, it's natural for you to confuse lust with emotion. I married you for the *castello*, and because I need a wife and heirs. Nothing has changed in that regard.'

Oh, God. She thought of the things he'd told her about fulfilling his father's dying wish and how the *castello* had felt like home. Meaningless platitudes. Humiliation was immediate and acrid in Chiara's gut.

She went cold as the true enormity of her naivety sank in. What for her had been a deeply transformative experience evidently hadn't been anything of the sort for Nico. How could it have been? She'd been a virgin.

Then something else struck her and she went even colder. She stood up, barely aware of the clatter of her chair on the stone floor. 'We didn't use anything...protection.' It hit her—she could be pregnant right now.

Something flashed across Nico's face. He said heavily, 'I know.'

Panic gripped Chiara, twisting her insides. 'You did it on purpose—you took advantage of my inexperience so that you could try and get me pregnant.'

Nico's face tightened. 'Your opinion of me isn't very high.'

Chiara waved a hand. 'Can you blame me? All I've seen is evidence of how ruthless you are. But even I hadn't considered you could be *this* ruthless.' She could feel hysteria building and had to breathe to calm herself.

Nico started towards her and then he stopped. Colour slashed across his cheeks and to Chiara's eternal shame, in spite of her anger and humiliation, she could feel her body yearning for his again.

'Last night... I wasn't thinking clearly. Of course I didn't intend for you to get pregnant. But as we are married, and I told you part of our deal was having heirs, it wouldn't be the worst thing in the world, would it?'

Yes, it would, thought Chiara. Because even though she knew she would feel a fierce love and protectiveness for her baby, she didn't want it to happen like *this*. In a confusing blur of lust and mindlessness. She hadn't intended for that to happen at all! And yet it had...

She said starkly, 'Last night was a mistake. It shouldn't have happened.'

'I never lied to you about wanting a real and practical marriage, Chiara.'

She backed away from the table, thinking of all the emotions that had been flowing through her the previous night. Thinking of how she'd felt when she'd woken. At peace. Sated. *Optimistic.*

Her grand plan that he would be in New York by now, realising what a mistake he'd made, lay in tatters at her feet. Thanks to her weakness and susceptibility. Her deep-seated wish to believe in some romantic fantasy.

'I should never have agreed to this marriage. It was a mistake.' Feeling desperate, she added, 'I want an annulment.'

He shook his head. 'It's too late. The marriage is consummated.'

Chiara's gut churned as suspicion turned to certainty. 'You seduced me on purpose.'

Of course he had! He was ruthless enough to cover all the bases. All he'd had to do was compliment her once or twice, make her feel as if she was the only woman on the planet, and she'd melted in a puddle at his feet. He'd played her like a fiddle, and her virginity had made it so much easier.

His expression was closed off. 'I seduced you because I wanted you.'

Chiara emitted a semi-hysterical laugh. 'Conveniently enough on our wedding night.'

And without using protection!

Nico picked up his tablet. 'My plane is waiting to take me to Rome. We can continue this discussion later.'

When he would undoubtedly try to seduce her again?

Chiara mocked herself. He wouldn't have to *try*. If he so much as touched her she'd go up in flames.

He started to leave the kitchen and then he turned to face her. 'Chiara, there will be many more benefits to this marriage than most. We are under no illusions about feelings and we both share a love for this *castello* and want to see it restored. The fact that we have chemistry is a bonus and will make this easier.'

And then he was gone.

Chiara heard the faint roar of an engine throttle and then silence. She sat down heavily in the chair and stared into the space he'd just left unseeingly.

She couldn't believe she'd been so utterly naive. And yet how had her life in the *castello*, being sheltered and overprotected, ever prepared her for something like this? For a man like Nicolo Santo Domenico?

She had to face the very stark fact that she'd merely replaced her parents as gatekeepers with her new husband, who clearly had no intention of letting her have a life outside the *castello*.

Her hand went to her belly again. *She could be pregnant. Already.* And she could imagine him greeting that news with a smug satisfaction that the Santo Domenicos were on their way back to domination.

All Chiara was to Nico was a pawn. And the worst thing about it was that he'd never tried to dress it up as anything else.

But last night had given Chiara a glimpse into another part of herself. She'd become a woman. And for a moment she'd believed there was something between them. She'd indulged in a vision of a *real* marriage. And she'd been utterly, astoundingly naive.

Last night might have been a sensual revelation for Chiara. But for Nicolo—no matter what he'd said about chemistry—it had to have been a very pedestrian experience. She'd given him a tool with which to coerce her to commit to this marriage fully. And that tool was her own weakness.

Chiara could see the future stretching out before her. She would be endured. Much as her father had endured her, disappointed that she wasn't a boy. She realised now that her fear of leaving the *castello* was far less than her fear of getting lost completely in the whirlwind of Nicolo Santo Domenico's life. Of finding herself pregnant and trapped for ever with a man who saw her only as a pawn. Never mind herself—she couldn't do that to an innocent child.

A sense of panic gripped her. *She wasn't pregnant. She couldn't be.* Life wouldn't be so cruel.

But she had to seize her chance now, before Nico came back. Before he touched her again and saw that he'd touched her emotions as much as her body.

She should never have thought she could manipulate Nico by marrying him. She'd underestimated him at every turn. She wouldn't make that mistake again.

CHAPTER FIVE

Five months later

'I THINK WE'VE found your wife, Mr Santo Domenico. I'm sending you over some pictures so you can see for yourself. She's in Ireland, working in a restaurant in Dublin. Also, there's something you should be prepared for... She's pregnant. When you confirm it's her you'll have her back within twenty-four hours.'

Nico's private investigator's words rang in his head. One word in particular: *pregnant.*

Nico got up from behind his desk and walked over to the window, which showcased a titan's view of Manhattan here at the heart of his global corporation which encompassed everything from real estate to media and tech industries. Enough to keep ten men busy, never mind just him. But his mind hadn't been focused on his businesses for weeks now. *Months.* Five months, to be exact.

He scowled, still incensed that his very meek and innocent Sicilian wife had had the temerity to leave him and disappear into the ether like a ghost the day after their wedding night.

His satisfaction that Chiara had been found was eclipsed by anger, because she'd put him in a very awkward position for these last few months. All his peers knew that he'd married, and yet he had no wife to show for it. His explanation that she was renovating the *castello* in Sicily was beginning to wear thin. Only a week before, at an exclusive charity auction, one of his adversaries had slyly questioned if his wife was, in fact, real.

Oh, she was real all right.

The erotic charge of their wedding night lingered in Nico's blood, much as he wanted to deny it, and the thought of having her back in her rightful place was precipitating a very unwelcome sense of anticipation.

For a man who didn't dwell on his past actions— and certainly none involving his lovers—their wedding night and the following morning had played ad infinitum in his head for the past five months.

Specifically, that first image of his wife naked.

That memory was burned into his brain like a provocative brand. He could still see the luscious curves, the heavy breasts, the tiny waist and full hips. Her hair long and wild. She'd looked like a beautiful nymph.

He hadn't considered that she might be so innocent, in spite of her being so unsophisticated. An anomaly in this day and age. It was no wonder that she'd been so affected.

But it had been a mistake to give in to his hormones like that. It had exposed him. And it was only because she was so inexperienced that she hadn't capitalised on his momentary weakness, like another, more cynical woman might have.

When she'd appeared in the kitchen the following morning and he'd seen the look on her face—shy, and still suffused with the same wonder he'd seen the night before—he'd felt a lead weight sink into his belly.

He hadn't tried too hard to refute her accusation that he had deliberately tried to get her pregnant because it was better that she think him capable of that rather than reveal that he had lost all sense and reason.

Coward... whispered a snide inner voice. He ignored it.

As much as he wanted their marriage to be a real and practical one, he didn't want her to develop feelings for him—because he would never return those feelings and it would make the marriage untenable. And so he'd left her under no illusions that there had been anything remotely romantic about their wedding night.

If Nico hadn't learnt to divorce himself from his emotions he would still be in Naples, hustling to make a few euros from stolen phones, or seducing rich and lonely female tourists.

He would never have fulfilled his father's dying request—to reclaim the Santo Domenico rightful inheritance and bring respect back to the name. *Finally.*

But now, even though he'd achieved what he'd set out to do—and much more besides, having created a vast personal fortune in the process—Nico couldn't rest. He had an errant pregnant wife to track down.

She'd left him a note, the contents of which were also burned into his memory—much as he didn't like to admit it.

Dear Nico,
As you will no doubt have noticed, I have left. I made a mistake in agreeing to marry you. We are not suited to each other. I only agreed to marry you because I felt it would be one way of securing my right to retain contact with the castello *and the burial place of my family.*

I think you would have to agree that you can find someone eminently more suitable than me. I don't want any of your money. I just want a divorce and access to the castello *a couple of times a year.*

Please take care of Spiro. He is old, and probably won't live much longer, but I'd like to think of him enjoying his last months in comfort. I've left instructions for his care and the details of his vet.
Yours,
Chiara Caruso

Chiara Caruso. Not Chiara Santo Domenico. As if they hadn't even married! And she cared more for that dog than him. That stung.

Her solicitor had got in touch after she'd disappeared, asking if Nico would grant her a divorce. He'd flatly refused.

What irritated Nico, though, was the fact that it hadn't been the possibility that she might be pregnant that had made him refuse—it had been a knee-jerk instinctive reaction. *He didn't want to let her go.* And he wasn't even sure why. He had the *castello* now, he could divorce and re-marry—someone eminently more suitable. Exactly as she'd suggested.

But Nico had never been good at taking other people's suggestions. Especially when he didn't want to do something.

None of the women he'd met in the last five months had interested him in the slightest. He'd found himself comparing their sleek thorough-bred thinness with the lush curves of the women he'd married.

Damn her.

Nico heard the distinct *ping* of a new email from behind him and went back to his desk. He sat down and clicked on the link. Images filled the screen. Images of his wife. Entering and leaving what looked like a small, intimate Italian res-taurant on one of Dublin's leafy city streets. The same kind of Italian establishment that populated cities the world over. This one was called Bella Toscana. Unoriginal and utterly pedestrian.

She was dressed in a black top and trousers and a white apron. He tensed as his gaze narrowed on the very evident swell of her belly. *Pregnant.* She'd be five months pregnant now. That small waist had stretched to accommodate her pregnancy.

Nico had always seen having a family as an abstract thing. A promise to his father. A duty to fulfil. A burden, almost. But now, as he looked at the image of his pregnant wife, he didn't feel abstract or dutiful... He felt a surge of something very primal. Possessive.

Mine. My seed.

Nico was shocked at this evidence that their wedding night had borne fruit. *If you're the father,* said a snide inner voice. Who was to say Chiara hadn't slept with another man just after him?

The thought of her sharing that look of wide-eyed wonder with another man made something even more primal and possessive beat through him. She wouldn't. But then...what did he know?

He barely knew her. But she had a hold on his libido he didn't like.

He ignored the snide inner voices and let the prospect sink in for a moment. *He had a family.* The revelation sent conflicting emotions through him.

He immediately thought of his father, heard his gruff voice... *'Nicolo, you have to have a family or our name will be gone for ever. You are all that is left of what was once a great and powerful dynasty. The Santo Domenicos cannot be allowed to fade away with such a stain on our name. You cannot let that happen... Promise me, Nicolo... Promise me.'*

And he'd promised him. Just as he'd promised him to regain the *castello*, whatever it took, along with restoring their fortune and good name.

Nico looked at the pictures again and focused on Chiara's face. She looked much the same. Her long hair was pulled back into a ponytail that swung over her shoulder. She still wore no make-up. She looked pale. Tired. That realisation made him feel uncomfortable.

He recalled the unusual light green of her eyes all too easily. And the way they had glowed like translucent emeralds as he'd joined their bodies. His gaze caught on her full breasts, pushing against the top she wore.

His body rose to rampant life.

Inferno!

He closed down the images and picked up his phone. When the call was answered at the other end he said tersely, 'It's her…yes. Definitely.'

Nico stood up again and walked back over to the window, the lingering heat in his body being replaced with icy cold resolve and anger.

'No, that won't be necessary,' he said. 'I'll go and get her myself.'

'They want the short pasta, Tony. Not the linguine.'

Chiara stifled a smile as the head chef scowled and made a rude comment about people not knowing how to eat Italian food properly. She put a hand instinctively on her neat bump, rubbing it distractedly. The baby hadn't moved in a while, but she wasn't concerned. It usually seemed to sleep when she was active, and then bounced around when she was trying to sleep—which didn't help her energy levels.

All she wanted to do was sleep...except sleep let the demons take over her mind. The nights were the hardest...when she couldn't block out the memories of *him*. Her husband. The man she'd left after one night of marriage.

One night had been enough to tell her that she was way out of her depth. She'd known she was out of her depth but she'd ignored the voices telling her so, too greedy to experience what he was offering. And it had burnt her. Badly.

She'd spent the first couple of months cursing herself that she hadn't tried harder to negotiate a deal in which marriage hadn't been necessary. Surely he would have agreed to *something* if she'd pushed him enough?

Now she'd never know. *And you would never have had that night,* reminded an inner voice. The night that had changed her life. Literally.

At first she'd tried to ignore the signs that she was pregnant—missed periods—telling herself it was stress. And it *had* been stressful. Her first time out of Italy, living in a foreign country with minimal English. But she'd done well, and she was proud of how she'd survived and thrived.

If you could call waitressing *thriving*.

She could imagine the scathing look her husband might give her. Because he *was* still her husband. He'd comprehensively rebuffed any overtures from her solicitor to agree to a divorce. *Why?* She kept circling back to that question.

And then her conscience struck with the other constant refrain. *You have to tell him about the baby.* She knew she did. Some time. But not right now. When she felt ready.

Heartburn crept up Chiara's oesophagus just at the thought of initiating a meeting with Nico. Coming out of her hiding space…seeing him again in the flesh…

'*Chiara*… Earth to Chiara.'

Chiara blinked and the restaurant came back into focus. One of her fellow waitresses was standing in front of her with her hands full of plates.

She jerked her head towards the door. 'Someone has just come in…can you seat him?'

Chiara lambasted herself for spacing out and snapped into action. 'Of course—sorry, Sarah.'

She grabbed a couple of menus and turned around to greet the new customer, planting a fake smile on her face. But it soon slid off.

Recognition was swift and brutal, because this customer stood head and shoulders above all other mere mortals. The menus fell out of her nerveless fingers.

It would appear as if she didn't have to worry about initiating contact with her husband. Because Nicolo Santo Domenico was right here. In the flesh.

Somehow Chiara managed to form some words. 'Can I help you?'

Those dark eyes flashed. 'I've found what I'm looking for, but I'll take a black coffee. Strong.'

Chiara's brain felt sluggish with shock. Her husband was here, in this small, unremarkable restaurant. *I've found what I'm looking for.* He'd been looking for *her*.

She could feel the simmering tension. The barely banked anger. She saw it in his eyes and fought against putting a hand on her belly, where his dark gaze had just rested. She'd felt it like a physical touch. Or the lash of a whip. Censorious.

She finally kicked into gear—before her boss came over to see what the stand-off was about. She picked up the menus and said, 'Of course.

Please take a seat and I'll bring your coffee right away.'

Nico was lowering his tall, broad frame into a chair as she turned away, her heart palpitating. She felt sick. Clammy. She was all fingers and thumbs at the coffee machine, cursing herself for not thinking more clearly. She spied the open back door nearby and for a second thought wistfully of making a run for it. But at that moment she looked back into the restaurant and caught her husband's eye.

He shook his head very slowly and deliberately. *Don't even think about it.*

Chiara finished making the coffee and carried it out from behind the counter, praying she wouldn't spill it all over the floor. She put it down in front of Nico with a clatter, belatedly taking in his pristine suit and tie. His clean-shaven jaw. Ridiculously, she found herself wondering if he had to shave twice a day or once? She'd slept with him but she didn't even know that useless information.

She was about to turn away when a large warm hand clamped around her wrist. The shock of his touch was blistering. A rush of X-rated memories filled her head, making her dizzy.

'Sit with me, *mia cara moglie*. It's been so long since I've seen you.'

Beloved wife. She was no beloved wife. She'd been a means to an end and she'd walked herself into the situation, believing that she could somehow emerge unscathed. She was far from unscathed now, at five months pregnant. And, as much as she knew this wasn't the ideal situation for a baby, from the moment she'd had to accept she was pregnant she'd felt a fierce love and protectiveness for her unborn child.

A child that didn't deserve to be born into this mess.

Anger rose and she welcomed it, pulling her hand and wrist free of his hold. 'What do you want, Nico? I'm working.'

He cast a disdainful look around the restaurant and then looked back to her. He said coolly, 'No wife of *mine* needs to work.'

Feminist hackles Chiara hadn't even known she possessed rose. 'I like working and I need to survive.'

'Because you ran away.'

'I told you—the marriage was a mistake.'

His eyes narrowed. 'Ah, yes, your kind note. I never lied to you, Chiara. I never pretended emotions were involved. I thought you understood it was a logical business agreement. A marriage of convenience.'

Chiara tensed. She was giving too much away. 'Yes, I did understand that. But I changed my mind.'

Now he was accusing. 'You married me just so you would be in a better position to negotiate terms?'

She sat down, defeated by Nico's presence. 'Can you blame me? You weren't giving me any options.'

Nico regarded his wife across the small table and felt the pull of desire in his groin. He cursed silently. He couldn't remain unaware of how lush she looked. Her breasts were bigger, straining against her top. And suddenly he thought of other men looking at her fertile body. Desiring her earthy beauty.

Because he could see it now. She *was* beautiful—in spite of her lack of adornment. She had stunning bone structure and a wide lush mouth. He had to fight off the memory of how swollen it had looked after his kisses. And those unusual light green eyes that seemed to change colour every second. They were like rare jewels.

He forced his attention away from her body and the desire she was sparking with an effort he resented.

He drawled, 'There are plenty of women who wouldn't consider marriage to me such a chore.'

Chiara sat back and folded her arms. 'Well, by all means divorce me and marry a more willing woman. I won't stand in your way.'

Nico let his eyes drop expressively to the swell of her belly. 'I think it's a bit late for that.'

She blanched, as if she'd forgotten for a moment. 'How do you know it's yours?'

Nico looked up again at her tart tone and assessed her show of bravado. It was all too flimsy. He felt the truth in his bones. This baby was *his*. A sense of satisfaction he couldn't ignore rippled through him.

'You were a virgin. I can't really see you hopping into the next available bed.'

She bit her lip and said, 'Maybe I didn't—but don't underestimate me.'

A cold fury swept through Nico at the thought of her in another man's bed. He said, with quiet but lethal economy, 'You will never be unfaithful to me, Chiara.'

Chiara felt the intensity of Nicolo's steely tone. A little shakily, she said, 'I presume that works both ways? Or am I to be subjected to a series of mistresses kept in luxury apartments in every major city of the world?' Though, she had to admit that the few times she'd looked him up on the internet since she'd left, he hadn't appeared with another woman. She didn't like to admit how relieved she'd felt.

'We are married. I see no reason not to remain faithful if my…appetites are satisfied.'

A sizzle of something hot arced between them and shock slammed into Chiara to think that Nico might— She shook her head mentally. She had to be imagining it—he couldn't *possibly* fancy her like this. She'd lost whatever small waist definition she'd ever had!

She'd never really believed him when he'd said they had chemistry. Not on *his* side, anyway. She believed that he'd wanted her enough to sleep with her, but no more than that. He hadn't felt the all-consuming desire she had.

The morning after their wedding night had shown her in no uncertain terms that he'd been as strategic about seducing her as he had been about everything else. Cutting off any chance she might have to escape their vows by claiming non-consummation. By not using protection.

Chiara opened her mouth to remind him of that, but then a shadow loomed over their table and she looked up to see her boss, a barrel-chested man called Silvano, who was also from Sicily. He was looking from her to Nico and then back to her.

'Your break isn't for another hour, Chiara.'

Nico stood up, rising to his full height of six foot three. He topped her boss by some inches, and the man immediately looked ineffectual. It almost made Chiara giggle, and she realised she was close to hysteria.

'Not that it's any of your business, but this woman is my wife and she no longer works for you. I have come to take her home.'

Her boss looked at her. He was a nice man, and he'd been quite protective of Chiara since he'd realised that she was pregnant.

'Is this true?' he asked.

She stood up, more conscious of her ungainly belly now than ever, and feeling very flustered after what Nico had just revealed. *He wanted her.* She hadn't been prepared for that.

She nodded reluctantly, knowing there was no way out of this. 'Yes, it's true. I'm sorry.'

The man shrugged. 'Mondays are always dead. If you need to leave I won't stop you… Unless you want me to?'

He shot a look at Nico, but Chiara didn't feel like giggling any more.

She avoided her husband's eye. 'It's okay, Silvano.' Her boss was a traditional Italian man, after all, and he no doubt welcomed someone turning up to claim her.

He stood back. 'Get your things, then. I'll send on whatever wages you're due if you give me a forwarding address.'

Chiara shook her head and felt a part of her lament that her brief taste of independence was to be over so soon. 'No, share them out with the staff. I won't need them.'

He put up his hands. '*Va bene*—whatever you wish.'

Silvano stepped away, and Chiara turned to go into the staff room at the back of the shop. A hand caught her arm and she reluctantly looked at Nico. He seemed taller and broader than she remembered.

'One of my men is round the back.'

He thought she was going to run again. She pulled her arm free and glared at him. 'I don't think I'd get anywhere very fast, do you?'

'How many women were sharing that room?' Nico's voice rang with condemnation.

He was referring to the room she'd been renting, in a big house carved up into numerous flats. Salubrious, it hadn't been.

'There were eight of us.'

'In bunk beds!'

'Rent is expensive in Dublin. They were nice girls.'

She fought not to sound defensive. They'd mostly been Brazilian students, in Ireland to learn English. And Chiara had found the communality of their living quarters—while not ideal, obviously—a novelty after living in the *castello* for so long, with all that space to herself.

'We looked out for each other and they helped me with my English.' She was proud that she was almost fluent now. She'd discovered an unknown aptitude for languages.

Nico made a rude sound, and then he said, 'If it had ever got out that you were there, living like that... You could have put the baby in danger.'

Chiara hid a dart of hurt. 'Don't pretend that you care about the welfare of the baby. All you care about is that you have an heir—which you planned all along.'

For a moment he said nothing, and all Chiara could hear was the hum of the private jet's engines and the soft muted murmurs of the staff at the other end of the plane. Then he turned towards her, and she could see his strong hard features tighten with some expression she couldn't decipher.

'The truth is that I had no intention of not using protection that night. No matter what you might believe about my ruthlessness.'

She was surprised he remembered what she'd said. 'What do you mean?'

His jaw clenched, and then he said with palpable reluctance, 'By the time we got up to the bedroom protection was the last thing on my mind. It's something I've never done before. That night... I wasn't capable of thinking straight.'

The fact that his tone was almost accusing led Chiara to believe him. She hated the betraying quiver of awareness deep down between her legs. He wasn't telling her he wanted her *now*. How could he when she looked like a beached baby whale?

Then he asked, even more accusingly, 'Would you have told me?'

Chiara's hand instinctively went to her bump, and his eyes followed it and then moved back up. There was a wealth of emotion she hadn't expected in his expression for a moment, before it became a stern mask again. And she wondered for a second if she'd misjudged his ruthlessness when it came to having children.

She took a breath. 'I know I wouldn't have been able to keep it from you. But I'm not sure when I would have told you...before or after the birth. I did believe that you deserved to know, at least.'

He frowned. 'What's that supposed to mean?'

'I was going to tell you that I fully intended

bringing up our child on my own. I still believe that a loveless marriage is not a good environment for a child.'

Nico turned to face her more fully. The awareness deep inside her grew more acute. He dwarfed the chair he sat in. And the whole plane.

'That family photo in the *castello* showed a seemingly content family, yet you admitted yourself that it wasn't all that harmonious.'

Chiara wanted to ask him why he was so cynical, but she felt suddenly shy. Which was crazy. He'd all but barrelled back into her life and kidnapped her! Even if she *had* come willingly. Because she really had no choice. Not any more.

'We weren't perfectly harmonious, no,' she admitted reluctantly. 'I was close to my mother, but after she had me there were complications and she couldn't have any more children. My father... He was disappointed he didn't have a son. He didn't think a farm was an appropriate place for a girl, so I wasn't allowed to get involved in the business, and then it all collapsed anyway.'

'Why were they so protective of you?'

Chiara felt like squirming under Nico's scrutiny.

He hadn't been so curious about her when he'd been railroading her into marriage. So why now?

Reluctantly she answered. 'I was sickly as a child. Nothing specific, but I was prone to picking up infections. I grew out of it, but by the time I did my parents were used to home-schooling me and keeping me close.'

She opened her mouth, then closed it again. She felt deceitful, but she really didn't want to admit that her parents' marriage hadn't been a truly happy one. It would only confirm his cynical beliefs.

A steward approached and interrupted with a discreet cough. Nico tore his gaze away from Chiara to look at the man.

'Excuse me, sir, but we'll be on our final descent into Rome shortly.'

'Rome?' Chiara asked when the steward had walked away. She'd only been to Rome once before, on an educational tour with her parents.

Nico looked at her. 'Yes, I've been invited to a formal dinner tonight, at the French ambassador's residence. It's the perfect opportunity to show everyone that my wife isn't a figment of my imagination.'

Chiara felt the lash of his censorious tone again. It made her hackles rise. 'I'm nothing to you but a pawn. You *bought* me along with the *castello*.'

'You allowed yourself to be bought,' he pointed out in a drawling voice. 'You wouldn't have lasted two minutes outside the gates of the *castello*.'

Chiara flushed at that. 'But I did last. I lasted five months.'

'Your place is by my side, as my wife and the soon-to-be mother of my child.'

Nico looked away from her then, and down at his palm tablet. Chiara felt like a child. As if she'd been summarily dismissed. She bit back a growl of frustration and looked out of the window as the plane landed in Rome.

The irony wasn't lost on her. She was fulfilling her fantasy of travelling and having new experiences while she'd never been more trapped.

'I didn't know it could look like this!'

Chiara stared at her reflection in shock. Her unruly hair was tamed into sleek shiny waves for the first time in her life. She had cheekbones. And full red lips. Her eyes were huge. She looked like a different person. Like the kind of person she saw in magazines.

'You have beautiful, naturally wavy hair, Mrs Santo Domenico, you just need to use the right products to make it look its best.'

Mrs Santo Domenico. The use of her married name broke her out of her uncharacteristically self-absorbed reverie. Since they'd landed in Rome it had been a whirlwind. Nico had been on his phone for the entire journey to his apartment, situated in one of Rome's most beautiful buildings, in one of its most exclusive areas.

He had the top apartment, with an outdoor terrace that offered breathtaking views over the ancient city. There was even a lap pool. And the Colosseum was within spitting distance.

On arrival, he had handed her over to a team of stylists to get her ready for the function. Chiara might have been insulted if she hadn't been so relieved.

She'd barely had time to draw breath, never mind let her new reality sink in. *Nico had found her and within four hours she'd been returned to Italy.* If she thought about it too much she felt dizzy.

'How many months pregnant are you, Mrs Santo Domenico?'

Chiara looked at the stylist, who had replaced the hair and make-up girl behind her.

'Five months.'

'Come with me. I've chosen a few dresses that should suit.'

As Chiara followed the very slim and sleek woman into a bedroom suite that had lots of wardrobe rails stuffed with clothes she tried not to feel totally intimidated. Her experience of shopping for clothes was via online bargain websites.

About five glittering dresses were hanging on a rail nearby and the stylist had started looking at them and looking at her.

Chiara said apologetically, 'I'm sorry I'm not very tall.'

The stylist smiled conspiratorially. 'Don't worry. Most people are about your height, and designers cater for normal women these days.'

Relief washed through Chiara as the woman pulled out a black dress and said, 'I think this one will be perfect. Try this on. I'll help you with the zip.'

Chiara went into the bathroom, and just as she was ruminating on her very plain white underwear, and how it would look under the dress, there was a knock on the door and the stylist handed her a box.

Chiara opened it to find the most beautiful underwear under layers of tissue paper. Black lace. And surprisingly practical. In exactly her size. Her cheeks flamed as she put it on, wondering how they had known her size. Had Nico told them? She wouldn't have credited him with remembering, but then she couldn't ignore the sizzle of awareness that had been between them since the moment he'd appeared in the restaurant.

When she was dressed she came out, and the stylist turned around and exclaimed, '*Bellissima*, Mrs Santo Domenico!'

Chiara didn't believe her, and reluctantly looked at herself in the full-length mirror. She sucked in a breath. The dress had a wide vee neck and then fell in soft flowing layers of chiffon to the floor. Her pregnancy was unmistakable, but the clever cut of the dress managed to flatter and make her look almost petite.

There was a knock at the door at that moment

and then a voice. 'Signor Santo Domenico is ready to leave.'

The stylist jumped into action, giving Chiara a wrap and a bag and helping with her shoes—a pair of black strappy sandals. At the last moment Chiara remembered her plain gold wedding ring and slipped it onto her finger. It was snug; her fingers had swollen slightly with her pregnancy.

And then, when she was ready, she took a deep breath and steeled herself to greet her husband.

CHAPTER SIX

NICO WAS HAVING a hard time focusing. He put it down to the fact that he had his wife by his side for the first time since they'd married and he wasn't used to being at a function with someone. But that wasn't it. The reason he couldn't focus was because when Chiara had appeared in the drawing room of the apartment a short time before she'd looked endearingly shy and uncertain. And...*gorgeous.*

She was a sleek and coiffed version of the woman who had walked down the aisle to marry him. Unrecognisable as the woman who had come to him that day in the villa in her boxy shirt and jacket and calf-length skirt. He wanted her just as much, if not even more, because he knew exactly what she was hiding under all that elegant packaging. A raw and earthy sexuality.

They stood amongst a throng of Rome's elite

society now, and more than one man's glance had lingered on Chiara.

Her hair was pulled back on one side and coiled over the other shoulder in a shiny Hollywood wave. The vee of the dress drew the eye to her creamy cleavage. Nico had had to restrain himself from demanding she wear something less revealing, because he knew that she was probably the most chastely dressed woman in the room right now. And yet he looked at her and all he could think about was sex and how his body ached for her. *Had been aching for five months.* He'd never denied himself the pleasures of sex for that long.

He felt almost angry that the neat plan he'd devised to marry Chiara Caruso had all but blown up in his face.

Her arm was linked in his and he realised she was gripping him so tightly she was almost cutting off his circulation. He looked down at her and could see naked terror on her face. 'Are you okay?'

She looked up at him and all he could see were those huge green eyes. How had he ever thought her nondescript?

'I've never been to something like this before. I don't know what to do or say.'

Nico's conscience pricked. He could see the faint shadows under Chiara's eyes. He'd whisked her out of Dublin, put her on a plane, and now she was here, at one of Rome's highest society events of the year. There weren't many who could swim easily in an environment like this.

And he could remember all too well what it had been like when he'd attended his first such event. He'd felt raw and uncultivated, and he'd been sure people were looking at him expecting him to steal the silver.

'When was the last time you ate?' He'd noticed that she hadn't eaten on the plane. In fact he noticed now that apart from her bump she'd lost weight. She looked delicate.

She blinked. 'Breakfast… I think.'

Irritation surged. 'You're not looking after yourself—or the baby.'

She turned to face him, pulling her arm free of his, eyes flashing. 'I'm not the one who arrived like a whirlwind and gave me hardly enough time to pack, never mind eat.'

Nico's conscience smarted even more. He

took Chiara's elbow and led her into the dining room, where the rest of the guests were heading. 'There's a five-course meal this evening so make sure you eat. Tomorrow we'll set up an appointment with a specialist and make sure everything is all right with the baby.'

Chiara felt prickly, and completely out of her depth. She'd never been in such an opulently decadent place before. Glittering chandeliers and hundreds of candles bathed the guests in a honeyed glow inside the huge ballroom of a medieval Italian palace—the home of the French embassy.

Chiara was nearly blinded by the jewels hanging off necks, ears, throats and wrists. Each woman was more beautiful than the last and the men were handsome and statesmanlike.

Sleek waiters in black and white uniforms moved among the guests with exquisite canapés and champagne.

It was seriously intimidating, and Chiara felt absurdly self-conscious in her dress.

Nico had looked at her earlier as if she'd had two heads. When she'd asked if she looked all right he'd just said a gruff, 'You're fine. We should go.'

She also felt far too jittery and far too aware of him. It was the first time she'd seen him in a tuxedo, apart from in photos on the internet, and she still hadn't got her breath back fully. How could one man be so distractingly gorgeous?

She was the only pregnant woman here. Every other woman was about a foot taller than her and the size of a stick.

'Everything *is* all right with the baby, if you must know. I was seeing a very nice doctor in Dublin.'

Nico made a non-committal sound. 'We'll still see a specialist here, and I'll make sure we have the best doctors available on stand-by in Sicily.'

They reached their table and Nico pulled a chair out for Chiara. 'I'm not due for another four months,' she pointed out as she sat down.

Then she noticed that Nico was walking away and a spurt of panic gripped her. Wasn't he meant to be sitting beside her? He took a seat directly opposite, but as the table was about six feet wide he might as well have been on the moon.

She noticed that he was in between two very beautiful women, a blonde and a redhead, who both seemed to be vying for his attention. She felt a spurt of dark emotion. Something she'd never experienced before—jealousy.

He looked across at her and raised a brow. She forced a smile, determined not to let him see how affected she was.

She felt very exposed and gauche, and at that moment a tall and very regal-looking woman took the chair on Chiara's right-hand side, while an ancient-looking man took the seat on her left.

To say Chiara was dreading the ordeal ahead was an understatement, and when the scary-looking woman asked, 'Well, then—who are you and what do you do?' Chiara's stomach fell to the floor.

She said truthfully, 'I'm no one important at all. I'm here with my husband—Nicolo Santo Domenico.'

The woman immediately perked up and looked Chiara up and down, taking in her protruding belly. '*Very* interesting. First of all, *never* tell anyone you're not important—because it's simply not true. Now, you must tell me all about yourself because if you're Santo Domenico's wife then I'm sure you have an interesting story... You know everyone used to call him "the man who can't be tamed"?'

The woman glanced across the table to where Nico sat and then winked at Chiara, saying, 'I'd say you've put the cat among the pigeons this evening, my dear.'

'What did Princess Milena say to you?'

Chiara looked at Nico, sitting in the back of the car in shock. 'She was a *princess*?'

He nodded. 'Princess Milena of Genoa. One of the oldest royal lines in Italy.'

Chiara absorbed this. 'But she was lovely...we had such a nice conversation.'

Nico sounded sceptical. 'She's famously taciturn and intolerant of people, and yet every time I looked over at you she was laughing.'

Chiara shrugged. 'We were talking about everything and anything.'

'Did she ask about me?'

Chiara raised a brow, intrigued by this glimpse of a less arrogant Nico. 'Paranoid?'

His jaw clenched. 'I went to her looking for investment once and she refused to see me.'

'She was curious as to how we met.'

'What did you tell her?'

'The truth…that it was through the *castello*. I see no point in hiding the facts. Obviously I didn't elaborate on the business end of our arrangement, but I don't think she believes it's a romantic match.'

'*No* marriage in that world is a romantic match. It's so rare you'd be more likely to see a unicorn at one of those functions.'

'I don't believe that. Why are you so cynical?'

'Because in my experience love is a myth peddled by writers, poets and artists to distract from the reality of life—which is that inevitably you're on your own.'

'What happened with your mother?'

Nico turned his face towards her. It felt as if they were in a cocoon as Rome flashed past them outside, its lights winking and fading.

'What's my mother got to do with this?'

Chiara heard the warning in his voice but ignored it. She was carrying this man's child. She needed to know who he was. 'A lot. She was your *mother.*'

'No, she wasn't. She gave birth to me, but that's about it. She left when I was only a few days old. Abandoned me and my father.' He sounded harsh and he turned away, presenting her with his profile.

Chiara's heart squeezed. She could hear the hurt in Nico's voice even though she knew he probably wasn't even aware of it. 'You never saw her again?'

He was silent for so long she thought he was going to ignore her question, and then he said, 'She turned up at my office here in Rome a few years ago, asking to see me. I refused.'

Carefully Chiara said, 'I can understand why you reacted like that...but she might have had something important to say...wanted to explain why she did what she did.'

He turned to look at her again and Chiara almost shrank back at the harsh expression on his face, lit up by the neon lights outside. 'I have no interest in her explanations, whatever they might be. She is dead to me. This subject is closed.'

She might have had something important to say.

Chiara's words scored at Nico's insides like blunt knives. He hated it that he'd felt compelled to respond. To say something. He hated it that he was now thinking of that day when his assistant had come into his office, frowning and saying, 'There's a Signora Santo Domenico here to see you—she says she's your mother.'

At first Nico had been too shocked to respond, and then a sense of sheer anger and hatred had rushed through his system so strong that he'd shaken with it.

He'd stood up and said, 'Tell her I'm not available and tell her never to return.'

He hadn't slept properly for a couple of months afterwards, and part of the reason was the guilt he'd had no control over. Exactly the emotion Chiara was provoking now. If anyone should be feeling guilty it was his mother, not him.

They arrived back at Nico's apartment and he felt wound up in a way that only one or two things could alleviate. Physical exercise or sex. He stood beside Chiara in the lift and saw how she was avoiding looking at her reflection in the mirrored doors.

'Why won't you look at yourself?'

She met his eye and he could see her blush. How could she blush? *Because she is still little more than a virgin.* That thought did not help Nico's levels of tension. Nor did the confined space, the scent of Chiara's evocative perfume or her lush body just inches from touching his.

'I've never liked looking at myself. And now... I don't feel like myself.' She gestured with a hand to the dress and styling. 'This isn't me.'

Tension made Nico's voice harsh. 'You're my wife—this *is* you now. You'll just have to get used to it.'

He saw how she paled when the doors opened. Nico felt dangerously close to losing the veneer of civility he'd grown over the years; dangerously close to the raw uneducated teenager he'd once been. All he wanted to do now was to lift Chiara into his arms, strip off that flowing provocative dress and lay her down, bare, on his bed, and then sink into her hot tight body and lose himself in oblivion until he felt focused again.

But she was pregnant. She was out of bounds. He had given her a separate bedroom. He didn't know if they could make love without harming the baby—this was uncharted territory for him. The fact that he found her even more attractive now was something he had not expected and didn't know how to navigate. He wasn't used to holding back.

She turned to face him in the marbled hallway, avoiding his eye. 'Goodnight, then.'

She turned to leave and Nico said, 'Wait.'

She stopped and turned around.

Gruffly, he said, 'You had Princess Milena eating out of the palm of your hand and she's one of the toughest nuts to crack. You looked beautiful this evening.'

A little flare of pink came back into her cheeks and Nico felt ridiculously light for a second.

'Thank you.' She turned around again and left, and Nico stood watching the empty space for a long moment. Then he went to his bedroom, found some sweats and went to the gym and exercised until he couldn't breathe. Then he took a cold shower.

Only then, when he was utterly exhausted, did he feel some of the tension leave his body.

'You looked beautiful this evening.'

Chiara lay awake for some time. She blamed the baby for starting its nightly Samba routine, but really it was due to everything that had happened that day.

That morning, waking up in the overcrowded

room she'd shared with all those girls, she'd never have guessed she'd be ensconced in Nico's luxury apartment in Rome by midnight. After having attended her first high-profile social event as a married woman.

In a way, she could admit that she was relieved Nico had found her, because telling him about the baby had been weighing on her mind more and more. And now it was done. The only thing she had to come to terms with now was how her life would fit in with his.

Did they have any kind of a future at all? Would Nico ever make love to her again? A shiver went through her, just remembering what it had felt like to stand next to him in the confined space of the lift. She was so *aware* of him. Would it ever diminish?

But as much as she craved his touch again she also feared it, because their wedding night had broken her apart—so much so that she'd had to put thousands of miles between them. If he touched her again, how would she be able to hide what she was feeling?

Her pregnancy didn't help matters. She felt as

if a layer of skin had been removed, baring her emotions even more.

Chiara put her hand on her belly and felt the baby kick. She couldn't stop a smile, even though she didn't feel like smiling. She hoped for their baby's sake that there was *some* kind of a future for them.

She just couldn't fall for him… Because if she did making a life with Nico would be excruciating. He was not a man who would ever love her back.

His attitude to his mother was chilling, even if she *could* understand how resentful and hurt he must have been after being abandoned by her. When Chiara had heard the pain in his voice earlier she'd wanted to soothe it. And that scared her because she should be remaining detached.

Then the baby kicked again and Chiara cursed herself for being selfish. As long as Nico loved their child, that was all that really mattered. She didn't want her child to experience what she had—feeling *less* than, or not enough. And that would be her priority—this baby. Bringing it safely into the world and ensuring that he or she felt loved and wanted, no matter what was going on between her and Nico.

'Do you want to know if it's a boy or a girl?'

The doctor looked from her to Nico and Chiara held her breath. She was flat on her back on a table, her belly exposed and smeared with cold jelly. They'd just been reassured that everything was fine with the baby. And now there was this question.

Chiara said, 'I don't care as long as it's healthy.'

She looked at Nico, who had been transfixed by the image on the screen ever since it had appeared. He looked pale. Then he said, 'I'd like to know.'

He looked at her. 'If that's okay?'

Chiara figured that for a man who ran a huge global enterprise, comprising myriad businesses and thousands of employees, it made sense for him to leave little to chance.

She shrugged. 'I don't mind.'

The doctor pressed down again on Chiara's belly and then she said, 'Okay, I just wanted to be sure... I'm delighted to tell you that you're having a baby girl.'

An instant sob of emotion came out of Chiara's mouth before she could stop it as she looked at the screen and saw the tiny heartbeat pounding away. *Her daughter.* She put a hand to her mouth.

It took her a second to realise that Nico hadn't said anything, and when she looked at him his expression was shuttered. Instantly she felt trepidation.

The doctor seemed to sense their need to absorb this alone and wiped the gel off Chiara's belly and pulled her robe down. 'I'll be outside when you're ready, but be reassured that all is well. Congratulations.'

The doctor left and silence filled the small room. Chiara pulled the robe down over her belly a little more and sat up. Nico was still standing beside the bed, dwarfing the small space.

Chiara forced herself to look at him. His expression was still a little shell-shocked.

A bitter sense of disappointment made her belly sink. 'You don't want a daughter.'

He seemed to come out of the reverie he'd been in and he looked at Chiara. He frowned. 'No... I mean...*yes.* I just hadn't really thought about it in terms of a he or a she yet. And now...'

He sat down on the chair looking a little bewildered. It was the first time Chiara had seen any kind of chink in his indomitability.

'Are you disappointed? Would you have preferred a boy?'

Of course he would, crowed an inner voice, *he's an Alpha male!*

But Nico shook his head slowly. 'No... I want the baby to be healthy, like you. It's just hard to get my head around. I think I'd just assumed it would be a boy.'

His honesty eased something inside Chiara. After all, neither of them had been prepared for this or expected it. Or planned for it.

She plucked nervously at the bedcover. 'My father wanted a boy. I mean, he would have been perfectly happy with a daughter as long as he had a son too, but then...when my mother couldn't have any more children...he was left with me. I felt the weight of his disappointment my whole life.' She looked at Nico. 'I don't want that for our daughter.'

He met her eyes. 'I will be the first to admit that my experience at the hands of women hasn't always been positive, but I'm not going to punish my daughter for other people's actions.'

There was something fiery in his eyes, and for a moment Chiara had a vision of him with a small dark-haired girl squealing with laughter on his shoulders. In a bid to stop him seeing the emotion she felt, she said, 'You said *"women"* and *"other people"*...what did you mean?'

Nico got up and paced in the small space. He'd taken off his overcoat and wore a dark suit with an open-neck white shirt. He oozed confidence and virility. Chiara hadn't been unaware of the lingering looks from the female staff of the private clinic, and it was probably only the fact that her doctor was close to retirement age that made her somewhat immune to Nico's charms.

Chiara wondered a little desperately how any woman could ever come to terms with being with a man like this, who would be in constant demand and the object of women's lust?

He turned around and looked supremely reluctant to speak. She sensed he wouldn't. So she said, 'Nico, we're about to become parents. I deserve to know who you are.'

He ran a hand through his hair, making it messy. It only enhanced his appeal. *Damn him.*

'There was a woman…when I was much younger. I thought I was in love with her.'

Chiara's heart clenched. He *had* believed in love. Once. 'What happened?'

Nico's voice was harsh. 'I found her in bed with my best friend and business partner. She'd encouraged him to betray me by doing a deal with a client behind my back and cutting me out. She overestimated his ability and severely underestimated mine. I cut them loose and went to America, and I never looked back.'

And now he was King of the World.

Chiara was realising that Nico might put on a cool, emotionless front but he was far from being that. He'd been hurt by his mother and then this woman and it had affected him. A lot. The fact that he'd once let a woman close enough to hurt him crushed something inside Chiara—the seed of hope that he would one day let *her* get close.

Quietly Chiara said, 'Not all women are like that…greedy and duplicitous. Our daughter certainly won't be.'

'If I hadn't met you I might still believe the worst of people, but maybe you're right.'

He came to the end of the bed and wrapped his hands around the frame. Chiara was acutely aware of his long fingers, recalling all too easily how they'd felt on her skin...*inside* her. Her breathing got faster.

Just then there was a knock on the door and a nurse popped her head around, her eyes gravitating naturally to Nico and then widening comically. 'Your doctor has another appointment scheduled but she'd like to chat to you before you leave.'

Chiara felt like saying something tart and snappy, to get the girl's attention away from Nico, but he just said thank you and barely glanced at her. He was oblivious to his effect on women, or else just so used to it he didn't notice any more.

He looked at her and she must have had an odd expression on her face because he said, 'What? What did I do?'

She shook her head. 'Nothing.'

He glanced at his watch. 'My plane is ready and waiting at the airport. It's time to go back to Sicily.'

He left the room so she could get dressed and Chiara felt alternately excited and full of trepidation about seeing her home again, never having expected to be returning like this.

The first thing Chiara noticed was that there were new gates—steel and reinforced. They opened automatically when Nico pressed a button in his sports car, which had been waiting for them at the airport.

As they drove up the driveway she saw gardeners working on the gardens. They'd been cleared and new plants put in. She immediately wanted to get out and inspect what they were doing, as her mother had used to love gardening before she'd got ill and the gardens had run wild. They'd even had a herb and vegetable garden outside the kitchen.

But then they rounded the last corner and Chiara's favourite view appeared—the *castello*, perched on the edge of the world, with nothing but the sparkling sea behind it.

She gasped. 'What's all that?'

'Scaffolding. The builders are almost finished doing the exterior refurbishment work.'

Chiara could see gleaming new tiles. For years they'd had leaks in various parts of the *castello*, but it had been way beyond their financial reach to try and fix them.

Nico brought the car to a stop in the main courtyard and came round to open Chiara's door. He had to help her out because the car was so low slung, and she hesitated before putting her hand in his, afraid of her physical reaction.

Nico scowled. 'I don't bite, Chiara.'

She flushed and put her hand in his, feeling it close tightly around hers. A wash of heat rushed through her whole system. She'd read in a book about pregnancy that increased hormones could make you more acutely sensitised to everything, including desire. *Brilliant.* She'd never felt more ungainly or more aroused.

It also hadn't helped to hear what the doctor had said to them before they'd left the clinic.

'I'm sure you don't need me to tell you this, but you're experiencing a very healthy pregnancy so there's no reason why you shouldn't be enjoying every aspect of your marriage—including the physical side. Some couples are afraid they'll harm the baby, but that's really just a

myth... You're in your second trimester now—this is when you can really enjoy being pregnant... before the last trimester sets in and it becomes a little more uncomfortable...'

Chiara's face had flamed bright red and she'd avoided Nico's eye the whole way back to Sicily, terrified he might be expecting her to jump on him and demand her conjugal rights.

And then a blur of fur appeared from around the corner, and Chiara dropped to her knees as Spiro all but jumped into her arms, whining with excitement and slobbering all over her. She laughed, but felt perilously close to tears to see her old friend and find that he was okay. His tail was wagging so hard she could feel the air moving.

In a very gruff voice she said, 'Thank you for looking after him for me.'

Nico didn't mention the veritable team of dog-minders and walkers he'd had to hire to keep Spiro occupied and cared for. He also didn't mention how the dog had somehow managed to burrow his way under Nico's skin, so that when he was sitting in his office and Spiro came in to lie under the desk at his feet he liked it.

'It was fine,' he said, and watched as she got up and walked away from him with one hand on the dog's head. She was more happy to see the damn animal than him. He felt irritated. She'd avoided looking at him or even talking to him the whole way here.

Actually, it had been from the moment the doctor had said that there was no reason they shouldn't be enjoying a full marriage. *Sex.*

He was one of those people who had thought it dangerous for the baby, but now... All he could think about was Chiara's lushly curved form and how badly he wanted her.

But evidently, if her reaction to what the doctor had said was anything to go by, the last thing *she* wanted was sex.

She wore the maternity clothes that the stylist in Rome had provided: leggings, a close-fitting clingy top that showed off her neat bump and a loose cashmere cardigan. Her hair was sleek and shiny. She oozed health and vitality and an innate sexiness he knew she was unaware of.

Once again it confounded him. He had never met a woman who didn't use her assets to gain some advantage.

She disappeared into the *castello* and Nico took a moment before following her, reliving the moment when the doctor had revealed the sex of their baby. *A girl.*

Nico, in his arrogance, had assumed it would be a boy. The thought of a girl frankly terrified him. But it also sparked a wave of protectiveness so strong that he felt tremors in his body. The only other person who had come close to sparking a similar feeling was Chiara, when he'd seen those pictures of her in Dublin. The evidence of her pregnancy.

Protectiveness. A totally expected and sane response for a man to feel for his wife and the mother of his child. It didn't mean anything more than that.

'I waited until your return before hiring interior decorators as I thought you would know best what to do.'

Chiara was shocked. 'I... Thank you. I wouldn't have expected that.'

Ever since she was small, she'd often daydreamed and imagined what she would do to the *castello* if she had the freedom and the money.

Her father had favoured heavy furnishings and dark colours, and her mother had gone along with it to keep the peace.

Chiara had even made a mood board of cuttings from magazines for what she'd like to do one day. Make the *castello* bright and modern and airy. Her mother had found her board and said, '*Piccolina*, don't let your father find that. But you're right, the *castello* deserves to look beautiful, so I hope you get to do this some day.'

Now, the prospect that she was actually going to get to fulfil her dream made her feel very emotional—especially since Nico would have had every right to get on with hiring an interior decorator in her absence after she'd left him. *Abandoned him.* Only now did it occur to her that what she'd done must have held echoes of his mother for him. She'd only reinforced his already healthy cynicism.

She looked at Nico. 'You must have some ideas?'

He shrugged. 'I'd like to retain as many of the original features as possible, while giving it a more open and modern air, but that's about it. I trust your judgement.'

The fact that his vision matched hers made her feel ridiculously pleased. 'But I might have awful taste.'

He gestured at the heavy dark curtains and furniture. 'Would you keep any of this?'

She made a face. 'No way.'

'Well, then, that's all I need to know.'

'Have you been living here?' Chiara asked, suddenly curious.

'Only for a few weeks here and there. I was in New York a lot. I've taken over your father's study—I hope you don't mind. And I've been sleeping in the master bedroom. *Our bedroom...*'

Chiara could feel the heat climbing up her neck and face again and cursed silently. She was hardly a blushing virgin any more!

She spoke fast, to detract from her self-consciousness. 'Of course I don't mind about the study. And the bedroom…the bedroom—' she nearly choked '—that's fine too. I can use my old room.'

There was a taut silence for a moment and then Nico said, 'No, *cara*, we will be sharing a bedroom. There's been enough speculation about this marriage without adding fuel to the fire. Unless that will be a problem for you?'

Chiara could feel her blood drain south while at the same time her pulse-rate tripled. A very disconcerting sensation. 'I can sleep in the room adjoining the master bedroom. It used to be a dressing room. That way it won't be so notice-able.'

Nico moved closer and Chiara's levels of panic spiked.

'What do you have to be afraid of? We shared a bed before...' He directed an explicit look at her belly.

Chiara was terrified that if she protested too much it would give away why she was so reluctant to expose how she reacted to him. While *he* was only insisting she sleep with him for appearance's sake.

'I'm not afraid of anything... I just don't sleep well at the moment. The baby is very active at night. I'll keep you awake.'

'Don't worry about me, *cara*,' Nico responded silkily. 'I can survive on very little sleep.'

CHAPTER SEVEN

A COUPLE OF hours later Chiara was still feeling angry and jittery at having been so neatly routed by Nico. *Sharing a bed.*

She'd felt a sense of complacency when she'd had her own room at his apartment in Rome. And now not even being back in familiar and well-loved surroundings was helping much.

She heard a noise and looked up from where she was stirring a pot at the gas stove in the kitchen.

Nico stood in the doorway, hands on his hips, frowning ferociously. He'd changed into worn jeans and a casual long-sleeved top, and it took all Chiara's control not to let her eyes drift and linger over his body.

'What are you doing?'

She lifted the wooden spoon, almost wishing she could smack him with it for corralling her into sharing a bed with him. 'I'm cooking dinner.'

'Where is the housekeeper?'

Nico had hired a middle-aged local woman—Maria—who had been bustling around the kitchen when Chiara had explored earlier.

'I told her she could go home for the evening. I usually cooked for my parents.' She was a good cook.

Nico came into the kitchen, still frowning. 'My wife is not a cook. That's why I hired a house-keeper and why you will be interviewing more household staff over the next few days.'

The fact that she was irritating him was some balm to Chiara's own irritation. 'I enjoy cooking. It's no problem.'

He came closer and seemed to sniff the air. She saw the flare of interest in his eyes before he could hide it.

'What is that smell?'

'It's *pollo alla cacciatora*. Not very original but one of my favourites.' She stopped, and felt a bubble of hysteria mount. 'I don't even know if you're vegetarian. We've never actually shared a meal…apart from last night.' When they'd been separated by a table wide enough for a football game.

Nico looked grim now. 'I'm not vegetarian.'

Chiara gestured to where she had set the wide wooden kitchen table. The place where she'd spent most of her time growing up—learning how to cook with her *nonna*, doing schoolwork, reading...dreaming.

She regretted setting the table down here now. It felt too intimate, all of a sudden. Too exposing.

'I thought we'd eat down here, but I can set the table in the dining room if you'd prefer.'

He glanced at the table and a look of something almost like fear came over his face before it returned to neutral. 'No, here is fine.'

Chiara served the stew into two big bowls and brought them over to the table. Now she *really* regretted not going upstairs, to the more formal dining room where Nico had undoubtedly been eating for the last few months.

Nico ate some stew and tore off a piece of the crusty bread that Chiara had decided to serve with it. The ultimate comfort food. Now she felt even more exposed. Nico would no doubt be assessing her and thinking that this was where her extra pounds came from.

But then he said, 'This is very good. How did you learn to cook?'

Chiara poured a glass of Chianti for Nico and sparkling water for herself. 'My *nonna* taught me. My father's mother.'

Nico ate more of the stew, and then glanced at her. 'How long were you without staff here?'

'For about the last five years.'

'That's a long time to be running a property this size on your own.'

She shrugged. 'We managed.'

He sat back and took up his wine glass. It should have looked ridiculously flimsy in his big hand but it didn't. 'And you really didn't know about the history of this place?'

Chiara dabbed at her mouth with a napkin and shook her head. 'No idea.'

She put the napkin down again and forced herself to meet Nico's eye.

'Although if what you say about my father turning your father away that time is true, he must have known. He was always paranoid about security and privacy. I think that was one of the reasons he insisted on home-schooling me even after I got better. Maybe he didn't want me mixing with the local children in case I heard something.'

'So you had no friends?'

Chiara felt as if Nico was pulling up a layer of skin and peering underneath to her tender underbelly. A little testily she admitted, 'Not really, no. I made friends with some of the workers' children, but their work was usually seasonal and then they'd move on.'

Nico said, 'When I was young I didn't have many friends either, actually.'

Chiara stopped her jaw from dropping. A man as dynamic and charismatic as him?

He grimaced slightly. 'Your father was secretive and overprotective—my father believed we were better than everyone else and that we didn't deserve to be where we were, in the flats of Naples. Other kids picked up on it and ostracised me. Jeered at me for believing I was better than them. Jeered at me for not having a mother. They knew about the Santo Domenicos and how far we'd fallen. It only made my father more determined that I'd succeed.'

Chiara felt a pang for Nico. She could imagine him as a scrappy kid all too well. Full of hurt and trying to hide it.

'I had one best friend I trusted with my life...'

'The one who slept with your girlfriend?'

He took a sip of wine and nodded. 'For years I blamed her for seducing him—she was very beautiful and knew how to use it.'

Chiara crushed a surge of self-consciousness.

Nico shook his head. 'But really it was him. I knew he had wanted her from the moment I introduced them. She just took advantage of his weakness for her.'

Chiara asked, as lightly as she could, 'Did you ever see her again?'

Nico avoided her eye and drained his wine. 'I've bumped into her occasionally. I believe she's on marriage number two now.'

He stood up then, and put his napkin down on the table. 'Thank you—that was delicious. Better than most restaurants I've eaten in. I have some calls to make... Leave the dishes for Maria. You don't need to do menial tasks, Chiara, not any more. And in future we'll eat upstairs.'

Moments ago Chiara had felt that black pang of jealousy, wondering if he still had feelings for his lover, and now she lambasted herself for it.

'Are you forbidding me to cook?' She forced a lightness into her voice she didn't feel.

'If I'd wanted you to cook I would have made you my housekeeper, not my wife.'

When Chiara woke the next morning she lay there for a long moment, soaking in the sounds and the smells and the warm breeze coming in through the open window. The earth smelled damp—it must have rained during the night. *The night. In bed with Nico.*

Chiara's eyes opened. The bedroom was empty—she knew that much. She looked to her left and saw the covers thrown back and the dent in the pillow where Nico's head had been. She could smell his scent.

She had gone to bed last night after dinner, hoping to be asleep before he retired, but not really expecting it to happen. Her head had been whirring with everything he'd told her, and the fact that they'd shared a relatively pleasant meal together. Until the end, when he'd more or less told her to stay out of the kitchen.

But after she'd washed and changed and scurried into bed, like a terrified little mouse afraid of a predator, she'd obviously fallen asleep immediately. Tired after her two eventful days.

The baby moved now, and Chiara put her hand on her belly, smiling. *A girl.* A pang of anxiety rose up though when she thought of Nico's response to the news. But, she had to remember that he'd been brought up by a single father after his mother had abandoned him, and then his lover had betrayed him. It was no wonder he felt less than enthusiastic about a girl. He wouldn't know how to relate because his experience of women was skewed.

Still, she couldn't believe she'd slept so soundly beside the man who had driven her mindless with pleasure in this very same bed on their wedding night. She put it down to extreme pregnancy fatigue...

There was a light knock on the door and Chiara clutched at the sheet like a terrified virgin. 'Yes?'

The door opened and a smiling Maria appeared with a tray balanced expertly in one hand. She came in and put it down on the table beside the bed. The tray contained orange juice, pastries, water, fruit salad...

Chiara stuttered a greeting. It had been a long time since housekeepers had served anyone in bed at the *castello*.

Maria was now delving into Chiara's cases, which she realised Nico must have brought up to the room at some stage while she'd slept. All attempts to tell Maria not to worry fell on deaf ears as the woman pulled out all the clothes that the stylist had packed and proceeded to hang them up or put them in drawers.

Chiara's belly sank. So much for hoping she could make some excuse not to sleep with Nico. Not only had she slept like a log, but apparently she'd be checked up on first thing every morning by Maria.

After Chiara had showered, and dressed in a pretty floral maternity dress, she went downstairs to find Nico. It felt strange in the *castello* now. But good. There was an air of activity that hadn't been there for a long time.

She found him in her father's study where, instead of her father's ancient computer, there was now a state-of-the-art desktop computer and two laptops. A TV was high on a wall in the corner, showing rolling footage of a financial channel.

Nico heard a sound and looked up. Chiara stood in the doorway in a dress that was all at once positively nun-like and yet more provocative than the most barely-there lingerie Nico had ever seen on a woman.

There were two straps showing off Chiara's toned arms and delicate collarbone. Her breasts were barely contained by the bodice, full and ripe. The dress had an empire line and flowed out over the bump and to her knees. Her legs were bare. So were her feet. And her nails were painted a coral colour that seemed absurdly provocative to Nico.

Her hair was long and loose, and he wanted to grab it and wrap it around his hand so he could tug her onto his lap, where she would feel for herself how hard it had been for him to sleep beside her last night while, unbelievably, she'd snored gently.

It had been a total novelty for Nico, to come to bed and find Chiara curled up on one side, already asleep, with the sheets pulled up to her chin. He had never slept beside a woman before without seduction and the pursuit of pleasure being involved. He'd half expected her to be naked and waiting.

He'd found it curiously disturbing at first, until he'd fallen into a fitful sleep, populated by

X-rated re-runs of their wedding night, and then woken with a raging erection as dawn broke outside.

Chiara had been on her back by then, one hand thrown above her head, the sheet down around her waist. Her chest had been rising and falling gently as she slept. Her thin nightdress had done little to disguise the press of her nipples against the fabric. It had taken all of Nico's willpower not to lean over and put his mouth there, encircling the peaks and bringing them to hard life... waking her up and seeing those green eyes widen with sensual appreciation and desire...

Instead he'd taken a cold shower and checked in on the markets waking up across the world, and now he felt thoroughly disgruntled and had no one to blame but himself.

'You slept well?'

Chiara nodded, her face pinkening slightly. 'Like a log. I must be more tired than I thought I was. In truth, the room I shared with the girls was like a train station—it was almost impossible to get a good night's sleep.'

Nico put down his pen. 'Why did you put your-

self through that? Why did you leave so suddenly? Didn't I at least deserve a conversation?'

The pink leached out of Chiara's cheeks and he
had the impression that she was ready to bolt. So
much so that he got up and took her by the arm,
leading her into the office and closing the door.

He let her go and sat on the edge of the table.
She was skittish, avoiding his eye. And then he
saw it—the delicate flush on her face, and the
pulse beating hectically at the base of her neck. A
surge of triumph went through him. *She wanted
him.* She might have slept through the night in
the bed beside him, but she wasn't immune.

'You owe me an explanation, Chiara.'

Chiara felt like a nervy foal. Why had she come
looking for Nico again? She cursed herself now.
She could be down in the kitchen baking a cake,
or checking on the herbs and vegetables. Or taking Spiro for a walk. Anything but this.

'I told you in the note. I thought it was a mistake for us to marry.'

'Why? You got what you married me for—
keeping your life at the *castello*. What changed
between the wedding and the morning after?'

Everything! cried a voice in her head.

And suddenly, in that moment, Chiara knew it. Somehow—pathetically—she had fallen for Nico, and she'd used the wedding night and their passionate combustion as an excuse to run. Not wanting to deal with the fact that she never would have allowed someone such intimacy, no matter what the circumstances, if she hadn't already been falling for him.

'I... I just changed my mind.' It sounded pathetically weak to her ears.

'After a night like we had? I remember how you responded, *cara*. What we shared is rare. Maybe it scared you a little?'

Chiara looked at Nico. He was so close to the truth that it shocked her. And it terrified her that he might realise. He was an astute man.

'Don't be ridiculous. I told you—I married you because I thought it would be the only way I could negotiate terms to keep access to the *castello*. I didn't marry you for...' Chiara felt breathless '...for what happened.'

Nico stood up, and he was so close now they were almost touching. Chiara had to tip her head back, and she was suddenly bombarded with memories of just what *had* happened. How good it had felt.

His eyes were intense. 'What happened,' he breathed, 'was amazing. I haven't been able to get it out of my head for the past five months. I've cursed you every night when I couldn't sleep, reliving that night.'

He was echoing her thoughts like a sorcerer. 'But you don't want me... How can you...?' She made a half-hearted gesture to her bump.

'Because you're pregnant?'

She nodded.

'It may surprise you to know that if anything I find you even more attractive. The sight of your body...ripening with my seed...is unbelievably erotic.'

Chiara wondered dimly how she was still standing. She couldn't feel her legs. All she could feel was an urgent spiking of delicious tension deep in her groin, where her intimate body was responding, getting hotter, damper. Aching.

'You want me, Chiara.'

It wasn't spoken as a question, but Chiara heard a question. She also saw something in Nico's eyes—a hint of uncertainty. She would bet that he'd never stood in front of a woman before and felt unsure if she wanted him.

Chiara knew she could lie. She knew he wouldn't push it if she insisted she didn't want him. She could blame the pregnancy. Step back and break the tension. Leave. But an excitement she hadn't felt in months was coursing through her veins, making her feel alive. *She didn't want to lie.* Or leave. She wanted to experience that sublime union again.

'Yes,' she said simply. 'I want you.'

A shudder seemed to go through Nico and he stepped up to Chiara, spearing his hands into her hair, tilting her face up to his.

'I meant what I said before…about the wedding night. I'd never wanted anyone as much. I wasn't capable of being rational. And I still want you like that…like a fever in my blood.'

He bent his head and claimed her mouth in a kiss that showed her in no uncertain terms the truth of his words. It was heady and intoxicating to think that he'd been thinking of her, wanting her. That she'd driven him to the edge of his control.

The kiss was all-consuming, and Chiara was

slipping down into a vortex of heat. She dimly wondered how she'd survived for all these months without this. The solid wall of his chest was under her hands and desperately, not even aware of what she was doing, she searched for buttons, undoing them, ripping them apart in a feverish desire to touch his bare skin.

Nico broke away from the kiss, breathing harshly. It took a second for Chiara's eyes to focus again. His shirt was open and her hands were splayed across his pectoral muscles. One of her straps had fallen down and her breasts were straining against the bodice of her dress.

They were so sensitive it almost hurt. *Now* she understood what the doctor had meant with that conspiratorial smile. Chiara's whole body felt like an erogenous zone.

Nico went over to the door and locked it and then came back, putting his hands under Chiara's arms and manoeuvring her so that she was sitting on the edge of the desk.

His eyes were so dark they glittered like black jewels. With his hands still under her arms, touching the sides of her breasts, he said, 'I need you *now*.'

She bit her lip to stop herself from sounding too eager. 'Okay.'

He kissed her again, moving between her legs, pushing them apart. The height of the table aligned her body with his perfectly. She could feel the potent thrust of his body through their clothes and, acting totally on instinct, she reached down and undid his trousers, finding him and pulling him free of his clothes.

He drew back, a breath hissing out of his mouth. Chiara looked down, and the sight of her hand wrapped around all that majestic masculinity almost undid her.

Nico caught the front of her dress and pulled it apart, baring her lace-clad breasts to his gaze. He pulled the straps of the dress down, found the clasp of her bra and pulled it off and threw it aside. Now she was bared to his gaze, and breathing so fast she was almost hyperventilating.

Nico cupped her breasts, his thumbs grazing her nipples. 'I've dreamed of this...of you...so many times.'

For the first time Chiara felt a pang of regret that she'd run. But then any coherent thought fled as Nico bent and sucked one hard nipple into his mouth, tonguing and nipping at the sensitive flesh.

Chiara squeezed the stiff column of flesh in her hand. She could feel the tension in Nico and knew she wouldn't be able to hold on. She was too close.

She took her hand from him.

He lifted his head and looked at her.

'*Now*, Nico.'

Nico reached under her dress and found her panties, pulling them off and down her legs till they dropped to the floor. He spread her legs even further and positioned himself between them.

Chiara was panting. On some level she wondered what on earth she was doing, sitting on Nico's desk in broad daylight, about to— But then he joined their bodies in a smooth but cataclysmic thrust and she didn't care about any of that. She only cared about *this*. The inexorable glide of his body in and out of hers and the exquisite climb of tension, higher and higher.

She pushed his open shirt off his shoulders, exploring his chest, wrapping her hands around his neck, pressing her body even closer. Nico put a hand under her bottom, lifting her so that he could go even deeper. Chiara bit his shoulder to stop herself from crying out.

Her belly was pressed against him and Chiara felt him touch the very heart of her as she shattered into a million pieces within seconds, every part of her pulsating and contracting as she drew every ounce of his own climax from his body.

They were sweating…shaking…breathing like marathon runners. When Nico could move, he extricated himself from Chiara's tight clasp and stood up. He felt dizzy. Undone. But also regenerated.

Her face was flushed and her hair was wild. Her nipples were wet and her breasts were pink from where he'd touched her and from the hair on his chest. She looked up at him. Eyes huge and dazed.

A feeling of intense satisfaction rushed through him. He couldn't even feel regret that he'd taken her on his desk like an animal. He'd never taken a woman with such urgency. *Not even her.* The thought was fleeting and he batted it away, not wanting to look at that significance now.

He tipped up Chiara's chin so she had to look

at him. Her eyes were too big, seeing too much. Nico felt exposed.

'There will be no running away again, *mia cara moglie*. And you don't need to cook for me and create some domestic idyll. I'm not interested in that. I'm interested in *this*, and in having you by my side when I need you, and in you being the mother of my children. *That's* why I married you.'

When Chiara woke the shutters were closed in the bedroom and the light was dim. She was totally disorientated. Her body felt heavy and lethargic. The baby moved and she put a hand on her belly—and then it all came rushing back, because she remembered Nico splaying a big hand across her belly and saying, *'There will be no running away again...'* and 'That's *why I married you.'*

He had married her to be his trophy wife... when she was the most *un*-trophy-like wife in the world. And to be the mother of his children. Not to cook or create a cosy domestic home. Which was exactly what Chiara had wanted to create here all her life, in this huge place that had always felt more like a mausoleum than a home. And that was because it had never been *theirs*.

Nico had left her under no illusions that things would be different now. He'd reminded her all too brutally, albeit pleasurably, of her role.

She rolled over on her side and then realised that she was naked under the sheet. She went hot all over, belatedly remembering how Nico had had to carry her upstairs to the bedroom, and how he'd laid her down, taken off her ruined dress, before pulling a cool sheet over her still tingling body.

She got up, pulled on a robe and opened the shutters, noticing the setting sun. She'd slept through the whole day. He'd put her into a pleasure-induced coma.

Feeling thoroughly discombobulated, Chiara took a shower and dressed in leggings and a maternity shirt—nothing that could be considered remotely provocative. She twisted her damp hair back and up and secured it onto her head with a clip.

When she went downstairs Maria was walking from the dining room. She saw Chiara and smiled. 'I was about to come and wake you. Signor Santo Domenico said you weren't to be disturbed till dinnertime. He's in the dining room.'

Chiara forced a smile while feeling out of place, because *she* was usually the one making dinner and serving it up. With a pang, she realised that that was unlikely to happen again. And then she mocked herself. She had to be the only woman on the planet who felt hard done by for having *less* work to do.

She steeled herself to see her husband again and went into the dining room. He sat at one end of the imposingly large table. There was another place set to his left, and Chiara went over and sat down. He put down the paper he was reading and watched her the whole way. She felt acutely self-conscious, wondering if he was thinking, *What is it about her*?

'You had a good rest, *cara*?'

Chiara felt prickly. He was so smooth. So used to these post-sex situations. 'Fine, thank you. You should have woken me earlier. I didn't need to sleep the day away.'

'Clearly you did. You've been overdoing it.'

Chiara heard the censorious tone in his voice and opened her mouth to say something, but a young girl came into the room with their dinner. A pasta starter. By the time she left Chiara had forgotten what she'd wanted to say.

She asked, 'Who is she?' as Nico filled her water glass and poured some wine for himself.

'She's Maria's daughter—helping out until we hire more permanent staff. Actually, I've arranged for someone from a local recruitment firm to come and speak with you tomorrow, so you can let them know what we need and the kind of people you want. We'll also need a nanny for after the baby is born.'

Chiara nearly choked on her pasta and put her fork down. This was what he'd done after their wedding night—made love to her with a zeal that had turned her inside out and stirred up all her emotions, only to behave as if nothing extraordinary had happened. And for him evidently it hadn't. He'd merely been scratching a physical itch.

Chiara knew she wouldn't survive unless she could channel the same kind of detachment—but not right now. Her anger bubbled over. She looked at Nico. 'I am *not* handing my baby over to a nanny.'

He put down his own fork. 'We will have a busy social schedule and I will expect you to be by my side. You'll be traveling abroad with me when I require it.'

When I require it.

Chiara's appetite disappeared. 'I am not your employee, Nico. I'll be the mother of your daughter and *she* will be my focus—not you or your career.'

Upset at this reminder that for Nico this marriage was very much just a business transaction, Chiara stood up and left the room as elegantly as she could, feeling Nico's eyes boring into her back the whole way.

She passed Maria, who gave her a startled look. 'The food...is everything all right?'

Chiara took her hand and said truthfully, 'It is delicious. I'm afraid I'm just not hungry.'

The women patted Chiara on the shoulder and glanced at her belly before saying something sympathetic about knowing how she felt. She obviously assumed Chiara had some kind of morning sickness.

Spiro appeared at that moment and came up to Chiara, nudging her thigh. She patted his head and then instinctively went to one of her favourite secret spots in the *castello*. The old library—a huge, cavernous room with hundreds of floor-to-ceiling bookshelves.

She pulled one of her favourite books off a shelf, as familiar to her as her own face, and then curled up in one of the big high-backed chairs and opened it. She was hoping it would help to give her back some sense of equanimity and control, when she felt as if she was in deep water and in serious danger of drowning.

Nico threw down his napkin and stood up. He'd just endured a hurt look from Maria after telling her he wouldn't eat any more dinner. He sighed. Since when had he grown a conscience and cared about people's feelings?

He took his wine glass over to the window. The view took in sweeping gardens all the way down to the sea. It was majestic. And *his*. Finally.

He should be feeling extremely satisfied right now. He'd achieved it all. But he *didn't* feel satisfied. He felt unsettled. As if the world to which he'd become accustomed, where everyone said *yes* and success begat success, just wasn't functioning any more.

Actually, there was only one area where he seemed to be misstepping all the time. *Chiara.*

He scowled, thinking of the dinner she'd prepared the previous evening. He'd literally never tasted anything better. And yet at every moment he'd resisted the urge to sink into that cosy scene with every fibre of his being.

The disturbing thing was how alluring it had been.

He wasn't stupid—he knew it stemmed from having grown up with a single father, and because their lives had been as far from a cosy domestic scene as possible. In a very secret place he'd always envied harmonious family units, so he'd told himself that it was all just an illusion, hiding the cracks in unhappy families. Something he would never indulge in because it wasn't real.

But it had felt real last night. Sitting and talking to Chiara…

Women had tried to seduce him over the years by creating something similar, believing *they* could be the ones to heal his fractured soul, but in every instance he'd walked out, earning himself a reputation as being cold-hearted. Impossible to please. Impossible to tame. As if he was a wild animal.

He'd felt wild earlier, when he'd made love to Chiara. She *made* him wild. She made him forget everything. She made him *want*...want things he hadn't thought of in years. Things he hadn't even known he missed. Or needed. Things that would make him weak. Make him lose his edge. Because if he didn't have his intense hunger to succeed and restore, what would be left?

And that was why it was important to keep her back. Make sure she knew where the boundaries were. *Make sure she doesn't get too close?* asked a jeering inner voice.

Nico ignored it and drained his wine. She would soon adapt to his life, he assured himself. She would grow used to the ease and luxury he could provide.

Her fierce assurance that their child would be her priority had made something dark spike inside Nico—something almost like jealousy. He told himself he was being ridiculous—that if anything it was a good thing that she felt so strongly about their baby.

Nico left the dining room and went to find Chiara. He was about to give up when he saw the door to the library partially open. He saw her straight away, curled up asleep on a chair, legs tucked under her. A book open, resting on her bump.

He reached down and picked it up. *The Collected Poems of William Wordsworth.* Nico put it down on the table beside the chair, and when Chiara showed no signs of stirring he reached down, slid his arms under her and lifted her up into his arms.

Chiara was wide awake—she'd been awake from the moment Nico had come into the room, albeit dozing. She'd actually sensed him before he'd appeared, the tiny hairs going up on her arms. Her body the traitor.

Now he was carrying her up the stairs with that awesome ease and strength. It took immense effort not to turn her head into his neck and breathe in his scent, reach out her tongue and taste his skin. But she was still feeling raw and insecure, and she knew if Nico seduced her again she wouldn't have the strength to say no, and then he would have chipped away a little more at the walls she had left around her.

So when he laid her down on the bed and pulled a cover over her she kept pretending to be asleep, and only opened her eyes when he'd left the room...like a coward.

The following morning when Chiara woke she was alone. She saw a sleek-looking mobile phone and a charger by the bed on the table with a note on top.

She picked it up.

Call me when you wake, Nico.

Chiara dialled the number that was on the note, and it connected straight away—almost as if he'd been waiting. A silly idea.

'Morning, *cara.*'

Chiara wished he wouldn't call her *cara*—it felt like a lie. She sat up and made her voice brisk. 'Good morning. Where are you?'

'I'm at the airport, about to fly to Rome for some meetings. But I'll be back this evening. There's a charity function we've been invited to in Syracuse. We'll leave at seven p.m. One of my assistants will meet you at the *castello* this morning to go over hiring staff, and also an interior decorator.'

Chiara desisted from saying *Aye-aye, sir,* and just responded, 'Fine, I'll see you later.'

She cut the connection and lay back on the bed for a moment. This was her new reality and she would just have to get used to it.

CHAPTER EIGHT

'THANK YOU SO MUCH, Carmela.'

The young girl smiled prettily. 'No problem. It's good for me to have someone to practise on!'

Maria's daughter was training to be a beautician, and she had helped Chiara to get ready for the function this evening.

She stood back now. 'You look beautiful, Signora Santo Domenico.'

Chiara grimaced, 'Please, call me Chiara.'

The girl gathered her things and left and Chiara sucked in a deep breath. She still wasn't used to seeing herself like this. Dressed up. The only time she could really remember dressing up had been on her twenty-first birthday, when her parents had taken her for dinner in Catania, just a few months before they'd died. Her mother had been so ill, but she'd insisted on going.

Thinking of the dress she'd worn made her

cringe now. It had been so old-fashioned and un-flattering. She could still remember the sniggers from a crowd of girls they'd passed.

This evening's dress was dark green, with a sweetheart neckline and a high waist just under her breasts. The top of the dress was lace, with a short lace sleeves. It was elegant and classic and it skimmed over Chiara's bump, which seemed to be getting bigger by the day now. Carmela had pulled Chiara's hair back into a low, sleek bun, and make-up made her eyes look huge.

She was just stepping into matching shoes when there was a knock in the door connecting the dressing room with the bedroom.

Nico came in, adjusting his cufflinks. He wore a white tuxedo jacket and a black bow tie, black trousers. And he was breathtaking. Hair still damp from the shower...

He looked at her and stopped moving, an arrested expression on his face. Chiara's whole body tingled with awareness. That black gaze raked her up and down, and then he met her eyes. She could see the heat in his gaze and it echoed the building heat inside her.

'You look…stunning, Chiara.'

Unused to compliments, she said, 'I… Thank you.'

And then he came closer and took a box out of his jacket pocket. A small navy velvet box. She looked from it to him, not understanding.

He made a small grimace. 'I know this was never a traditional marriage, but I should have given you an engagement ring. I'd like to rectify that now.'

He opened the box and Chiara looked inside and gasped. It was a beautiful emerald, baguette cut, with smaller diamonds either side.

He took it out and held it up. 'Shall we see if it fits?'

Feeling a prickle of superstition, and almost hoping it wouldn't fit because that might mean something and it was too beautiful, Chiara held her hand out. Nico took it and slid the ring down her finger so it nestled alongside her wedding band. Her heart clenched. It fitted perfectly.

Weakly she said, 'You shouldn't have bought this. It must have cost a fortune.'

Nico's hand tightened on hers and she looked up at him. He was shaking his head.

'Seriously? Most women would be asking for a bigger gem.'

Chiara felt gauche. Stiffly she said, 'I'm not most women.'

'No,' Nico said, 'you're not.'

Chiara pulled her hand back, avoiding Nico's dark eyes that seemed to see too much. 'It matches my dress.'

'It matches your eyes.'

Chiara looked at Nico again and the electricity flowed between them. A delicious coil of tension knotted deep down inside her.

Nico took a step towards Chiara and she saw the intent in his eyes. She could feel herself softening, moving towards him almost helplessly, as if he were a magnet. But she put her hands up to his chest, saw the emerald glinting in her peripheral vision like a beacon. A reminder not to let him get too close.

'Wait…my make-up…' she said half jokily. 'I'll never be able to re-do it on my own.'

Nico's jaw clenched. 'You don't need make-up. But you're right—we should leave.'

Chiara followed him out, feeling wobbly in the high heels after what Nico had said. Did he mean she didn't need make-up in a *good* way? Or because it didn't make any difference? But then she thought of how he'd just looked at her and her heart skipped a beat. Maybe he meant it in a good way.

A driver was waiting to chauffeur them the short distance to Syracuse, and as Chiara slid into the luxurious confines of the back of the car she realised that she couldn't keep pushing Nico back for ever. She would have to learn how to disguise the way she felt when he touched her or she wouldn't survive this marriage.

'Don't *touch* me. You disgust me.'

Chiara tried not to let her jaw drop as the very tall, very glamorous woman they'd just been talking to, with her husband, stalked away and into the crowd. She and her husband had just had a very brief but vitriolic row, sparked off by him making a snide remark about her shopping habits.

Her husband, an equally tall, grey-haired gentleman, didn't even look surprised. He said lightly, 'Excuse my wife. She likes to air our grievances in public—it adds an extra dimension to the torture that is our marriage.'

He walked away, leaving Nico and Chiara staring after him. Chiara was in shock. When she looked at Nico, though, he didn't appear to be too perturbed.

'That was...*horrible.*'

The whole time they'd been talking there had been a brittle tension between the couple. And the wife had flirted outrageously with Nico, precipitating her husband's snide remark.

Nico looked down at her. 'Was it? Maybe they were just being more honest than most of the people here who can't stand each other. They're probably already re-enacting that exact scenario they just played out with us. Couples like that get off on public displays of aggression.'

Chiara shivered. She felt cold all of a sudden. And disheartened by Nico's persistent cynicism. The room was too hot and Chiara saw open French doors nearby. Muttering something about needing air, she put her glass of water down and made her way through the glitterati of Syracuse.

When she got outside the terrace was mercifully empty and a cool breeze was coming in off the ocean in the distance. It was dusk and lights were twinkling on, lighting up the stunning Syracuse cathedral nearby. It was magical. *Romantic.*

Chiara put her hands on the stone wall and looked down at her ring, glittering as brilliantly as the rest of the jewels she'd seen in the room. Was that why Nico had given it to her? To keep up with his peers? Had he noticed that Chiara wasn't adorned enough?

Here she was, married, with a beautiful engagement ring and pregnant. She'd always imagined in this scenario that she'd be with someone she loved. Who loved her. She'd seen the lack of love between her parents and had always yearned for something more. That was why she'd devoured romances all her life, stuffing them behind other books in the library so her father wouldn't find them.

Was it really asking too much to love and be loved in return? She hated it that the world Nico moved in seemed to be populated by cynical people.

She sensed him behind her and tensed, not ready to see him. But when was she *ever* ready?

'Are you okay?'

There was concern in his voice and Chiara

turned around. She waved a hand. 'I'm fine—it was getting stuffy in there.'

His eyes dropped to the swell of her belly. 'We need to set you up with a doctor—we'll do it tomorrow.'

She put a hand on her belly. 'I'm fine.'

The baby gave a vigorous kick at that precise moment and Chiara let out a little *oof.*

Immediately Nico put his hands on her arms. 'What is it? The baby?'

Chiara shook her head, something quivering inside her at the concern in his voice, even if it *was* only for the baby.

'She's moving.' Acting on instinct, Chiara reached for Nico's hand and placed it firmly on her belly, with her own hand on top. 'She'll do it again…just wait.'

It seemed very important to Chiara right then that Nico should experience this moment, amidst all the cynicism, and feel something very *un-*cynical and pure. His daughter.

For a heart-stopping moment nothing happened. Chiara was about to apologise but then the baby kicked again, even harder. As if she *knew.*

Chiara held her breath as a look of pure wonder came over Nico's face and his eyes widened on hers. Her chest swelled and she felt a swooping sensation. He was *getting* it. The baby kicked again and Chiara couldn't help a small laugh escaping. Pure joy in the moment. In new life. In *hope* that maybe, just maybe—

'Well, well, isn't *this* a cosy scene.'

Nico's whole body went rigid and he lifted his hand off Chiara's bump. Chiara looked to her right, to see one of the most beautiful women she'd ever seen in her life. Flawless bone structure, enviably smooth olive skin, full pouting lips and long sleek black hair. She was poured into a midnight-blue glittering gown that was slashed all the way to her navel, displaying the perfect globes of her breasts.

Her dark and dramatically kohled eyes were on Chiara—specifically on her bump. 'Ingenious...' she purred. 'To trap Nico by getting pregnant. Maybe I should have thought of that myself.'

And suddenly Chiara knew who this was. *The woman who had broken Nico's heart.* How could she not have? She was perfection.

'That's enough, Alexandra. Chiara does not deserve your spite.'

Nico's voice was taut with anger, but that did little to assuage Chiara's growing sense of insecurity.

The woman wouldn't stop looking at Chiara, her dark eyes raking her up and down. 'Are you seriously telling me that you *chose* to be with this woman? I can't believe you could bring yourself to—'

'Enough!'

Nico's voice rang out like a pistol shot. But Chiara put up her hand when she thought he was about to say something else. His ex-lover's words were cutting far too close to the bone for Chiara's liking, but she wasn't going to stand meekly by and let Nico defend her.

She was blisteringly angry that a precious moment had been ruined—infected by the cynicism she hated so much.

Chiara walked up to the woman—so close that her belly was almost touching her. She had to look up because she was so much smaller, and some part of her delighted in seeing the woman swallow nervously.

'My marriage to Nico is none of your business. You gave up any right to know *anything* about my husband when you slept with his best friend. You are not a nice person. And yet I wish you well, because everyone deserves a chance.'

Before Chiara could lose her nerve, she turned and walked back into the party, through the throng and all the way down to the foyer, which was empty. She paced there for a few moments, sucking in deep breaths to try and diminish the rush of adrenalin.

Nico appeared at the top of the stairs and Chiara watched him come down. His face was expressionless, but then when he got closer she saw that there was a small smile playing around his mouth.

'Well, I think you handled Alexandra pretty well. But you didn't really need to jump to my defence.'

'I didn't want you to jump to *my* defence. I'm not sorry about what I said.'

Nico's smile faded. 'You shouldn't be. She owes you an apology. She was unbelievably rude.'

Chiara looked at the wide marble stairs behind him. 'Do we have to go back in there?'

Nico almost shuddered. 'God, no. I'm done.' He surprised her by taking her hand. 'Are you tired?'

There was still too much adrenalin pumping around Chiara's body. She shook her head.

'Good. I'd like to show you somewhere—it's not far.'

Chiara groaned appreciatively. 'This is amazing.'

'I know. Have you ever tasted better gelato than this?'

She shook her head, then said with a rueful smile, 'But I haven't exactly travelled a lot.'

'You'll have plenty of opportunities to travel with me.'

Chiara looked at him. 'We'll have to see how that works with the baby... I'm not leaving her for any length of time, Nico.'

He took a sip of his espresso and inclined his head. 'I know, and I have to commend you for it. I haven't had the benefit of selfless maternal love, so I'll have to trust your judgement.'

'I'm sorry that you didn't know your mother.'

Nico shrugged. 'You can't miss what you don't know.'

Chiara did not agree, but she didn't want to shatter the peace so she took another piece of ice cream, relishing its tart lemon taste as it slipped down her throat. The gelato parlour was right on the seafront and very busy, mainly with groups of laughing joking teenagers.

Nico had given Chiara his jacket against the breeze coming in off the sea, so she sat there now under the fluorescent lights in his jacket and her evening dress. She loved it. And she loved it that he had brought her here, away from that stuffy party. Away from *her*.

'How did you know about this place?'

Nico looked around. 'My father told me about it. He used to come here on boat trips from Calabria with his father when he was small.'

They sat in silence for a moment as the gang of teenagers moved off down the seafront. Chiara envied them their light-hearted ease and friendship.

Nico put down his small espresso cup and leaned forward. He had undone his bow tie and opened the top button of his shirt. He looked rakish and sexy.

'I know you want more, Chiara.'

Chiara looked at him, shocked. Had he seen into her mind?

'I saw your collection of romance novels, hidden behind other books in the library. Unless they were your mother's?'

Chiara knew she could laugh breezily and lie, but she didn't want to. 'Yes, they're mine. What do you mean by knowing I want more?'

'Just that I think you were hoping for love... and romance. Not a marriage of convenience.'

Chiara shrugged and played with her ice cream spoon. She was terrified he'd make the link between her running away after their wedding night and her deepest most secret dreams. Nonchalantly she said, 'I'm not a total fantasist, Nico. I know life doesn't always turn out how you expect it to.'

He sighed. 'I just wanted to say that while I can't give you everything you want, I promise to do my utmost to make you as happy as I can.'

Chiara looked at him, and the little flame of hope that had sprung up when he'd felt the baby kicking withered a little inside her.

'I appreciate that.'

'I like you, Chiara. I respect you... You helped me to achieve a long-held ambition and dream— to restore the *castello* to the Santo Domenico name. You're giving me a child. We have insane chemistry, and we want each other—which is more than can be said for a lot of those couples we saw at the party this evening. I think we have a lot going for us. I think we can be happy.'

Chiara sucked in a deep breath. She hadn't been expecting Nico to be so honest. It was heartening and also quietly devastating. He was telling her not to get her hopes up. Not to wish for more.

That woman Alexandra had hurt him a long time ago, and maybe seeing her again this evening had reinforced his own walls of defence. They were impenetrable.

What could she say? Except, 'Okay...we'll do our best to make it work.'

Nico reached across the table and took her hand, lacing his fingers through hers. In spite of the heaviness in her heart Chiara felt the familiar burn of desire and saw it in his eyes too. She knew that no matter what he said, or how hard she tried, that little flame of hope wouldn't die out completely...not yet.

Her emerald engagement ring glinted at her mockingly and Chiara turned her hand away so she couldn't see it.

* * *

Chiara had taken off her shoes in the car on the way back and when they reached the *castello* Nico insisted on carrying her from the car, in spite of her sleepy protests. But by the time they reached the bedroom Chiara was wide awake— and very aware of Nico, and the way his jaw was stubbled after a day's growth.

Nico put her down and turned on a couple of lamps—just enough to see. He came and stood behind her in front of the mirror, where she was trying to reach the back of the dress.

'Let me.'

She took her hands down and felt him find the zip and pull it down to just above her buttocks. She shivered minutely.

'Cold?' he asked disingenuously. It was the height of summer.

She wanted to scowl, but when she looked at him in the mirror her heart stopped. He was so dark...and towering over her. She shook her head.

He smirked. 'I didn't think so.'

He pushed the dress off her shoulders and then tugged it all the way over her hips, so it fell to the floor in a *swish* of silk and chiffon. Now she wore only a strapless bra, that barely contained her breasts, and panties.

Nico undid her bra and that fell away too, releasing her breasts. Chiara wanted to turn her head away, but she couldn't take her eyes off him. He was bending his head now, pressing a kiss to where her neck met her shoulder, and she shuddered as a wave of desire raced through her body.

He stood up and put his hands on her shoulders. 'Look at yourself, *cara*, you're beautiful.'

Reluctantly, Chiara looked at herself, and watched Nico undo her hair and loosen it so that it fell over one shoulder, almost touching her breast.

His hands came around and cupped her breasts and she caught her breath. She could see her nipples peak into hard points, her skin flushing with arousal.

Her belly was a perfect rounded curve and Nico's hand moved down, over her belly and lower, under her underwear. She couldn't breathe.

'Keep looking at yourself.'

It was a command that Chiara had to obey. One of Nico's hands was on her breast, kneading the tender flesh, finding a nipple and tweaking it, and his other hand was between her legs, fingers seeking and exploring right into the heart of her, where she was hot and damp and aching.

Her legs opened to give him more access. She groaned and bit her lip, unable to take her eyes off what he was doing to her. He was winding her tighter and tighter, his clever, merciless fingers moving in and out until she couldn't stop a gasp of shock as she exploded in a spasm of pleasure so intense her legs turned to jelly.

Nico finally turned her quivering body around and hauled her into him before kissing her sense-less.

After a long moment, when she aftershocks of pleasure had finally diminished, Nico pulled back. He smoothed Chiara's hair back from her brow and said, 'See? This…this is all we need.'

Chiara was too spent to argue, and when he laid her down on the bed and pulled the sheet over her she let sleep claim her, obscuring the fact that she knew pain would be an inevitable part of liv-ing with Nico because she was in love with him.

Nico looked down at Chiara sleeping, and even though his own body throbbed with sexual frustration he didn't mind. It had been intensely erotic, watching her fall to pieces around his hand and fingers like that, through the mirror.

Seeing Alexandra earlier had been a shock. It was always a shock. Except this time Nico had truly resented her intrusion on a private moment. And when she'd started to attack Chiara it had taken him a couple of seconds to realise that Chiara had stepped up to her, confronted her. He hadn't noticed because he'd been so blinded by rage.

A kind of rage he couldn't remember feeling before. Not even when he'd found Alexandra in bed with his friend.

No one had ever defended Nico like that.

He could remember being beaten by a group of lads when was a young teenager. His father had found him, bruised and bleeding on the ground, with the boys standing around him jeering. His father had just stood there and said, *'Get up, boy. You're a Santo Domenico. Show them!'*

And Nico had somehow hauled himself up and limped home.

When Chiara had walked away earlier, Nico had been aware of a load lifting off his chest. As if he'd finally broken free of some shackle. He'd barely even glanced at Alexandra's stricken face as he'd gone after his wife.

His wife. His lover. The mother of his child.

Nico felt a surge of protectiveness race through him. He knew he couldn't give Chiara everything she wanted—not even for *her* was he willing to expose himself to the vulnerability of loving someone again. Seeing Alexandra was a sign he couldn't and wouldn't ignore.

But he and Chiara had all they needed. They didn't need anything deeper.

CHAPTER NINE

CHIARA FLIPPED ONTO her back and lazily moved her arms and legs, just enough so that she didn't sink like an overinflated beach ball to the bottom of the pool. It was late summer and she loved the evenings, when the intense heat was lessening and she could go down to the newly installed infinity pool and cool off.

She looked up into the azure blue sky. There was only the sound of the sea water lapping against the shore nearby, and the call of the birds. The workmen restoring the outside of the *castello* had finished for the day, as had the interior decorators, who were moving through the *castello* room by room, accompanied by someone from the Italian National Heritage Trust to make sure none of the original features were damaged.

Chiara sighed. She felt…*restless*. In spite of the soothing surroundings. Content…but not happy. And then she castigated herself. She had it so

much better than many people. She had no reason to complain.

Her husband was unfailingly solicitous. He was
considerate. He never spent more than three days
away from home. And when he was at home...
Chiara blushed even now to think of how intense
the attraction still was between them. In spite of
her pregnancy.

Since she'd turned eight months pregnant he'd
decided not to go back to New York for work
until after the baby was born, and he'd promised
that once Sofia was old enough to travel they
would all go as a family.

Sofia.

They'd already agreed on the name.

Sofia, after Chiara's beloved *nonna*.

Maria was now living in at the *castello*, along
with two other permanent household staff. Chiara
had little to worry about except for the fact that
no matter how considerate Nico was, how solicitous, it was as if a glass wall separated them. She
could get close, but not too close. He maintained
a distance that she couldn't seem to breach, no
matter what.

The only time she seemed to get closer to the

man behind the wall was when they made love. No matter how 'pregnant' Chiara was feeling— fatigued, et cetera—as soon as she laid eyes on Nico it all fell away and she became a mass of needy hormones.

'*Here* you are…'

Chiara stopping moving in the water and promptly sank like a stone. She popped up again quickly, spluttering and blinking to clear her eyes of water, to see that Nico's voice hadn't been an aural hallucination. He was standing at the side of the pool in short swimming trunks, holding a towel and looking too gorgeous for words.

It was so unfair. As her body got progressively rounder, his body remained as beautiful as ever. Lean and hard-muscled. Not an ounce of spare fat. And that tantalising hair on his chest, leading down to the line dissecting his six-pack and then disappearing—

Chiara forced her eyes up to see an amused expression on his face. She scowled. He was disturbing her peace. 'You're back early.' He hadn't been due back from Rome till tomorrow.

An expression she couldn't decipher crossed his face fleetingly before he dropped the towel and dived gracefully into the pool, surfacing just inches away from Chiara.

Predictably, her body was already responding, tingling. Every cell was aligning with his, like magnet filings finding true north. He reached for her, his hands finding her arms and pulling her towards him until her belly touched his.

She put her hands on his arms, feeling the muscles bunching under his skin. He smiled and it made him look ten years younger. Carefree.

'You *can* admit you're pleased to see me.'

When he was like this—charming—it was almost impossible to forget that she had to keep her guard up: the final bastion of her self-protection.

'Fine,' she conceded. 'It's nice to have you home.'

He winced. '*Nice?* Now, that is *not* a word levelled at me too often.'

Chiara's legs touched his as she trod water. He didn't have to—he was so tall. He started to move backwards, though, taking her with him as he moved down the pool.

'Nico…' She groaned, hating it that he could manipulate her so easily.

He ignored her, lazily pulling her along as if

she was learning how to swim. Chiara gave up and let him tug her. She could feel the damp tendrils of hair where they'd fallen out of her high bun, clinging to her cheeks.

And then he stopped and stood, and Chiara could stand too, now it was shallow enough. He looked at her for a long moment, and there was something almost desperate in his gaze that made Chiara's heart hitch, but then it was forgotten when he kissed her, and tingling awareness exploded into full-on arousal.

Nico's hands traced Chiara's body through the swimsuit, cupping her breasts, her bottom. She ached for him. Every time. He walked her back to the wall and she leant against it, looking up at him, breathing fast. Her peace was well and truly shattered, but she didn't care any more.

He looked down at her, rivulets of water running down his chest and face, hair flopping forward damply, making him look endearingly young.

She could feel him against her. Hard. Potent. She reached down under the water and pulled down his shorts, taking him in her hand. It was the only time she felt marginally powerful in this relationship—when he looked at her as he was looking at her now, slightly dazed. Flushed.

'Turn around,' he said.

She took her hand from him, turning around to face away from the house out towards the sea beyond. Her heart was drumming with excitement. He peeled the straps of her bathing suit down and freed her breasts, reaching around to cup them and tease them to hard, aching points.

Chiara leant her head back against him. She sensed his desperation as he pulled down her suit over her hips and her legs. He was naked behind her, and then he was pushing her legs apart, pulling her back so that he could thrust into her in one smooth but cataclysmic thrust.

Her body clenched around him in need as he slowly began to thrust in and out, building up an inexorable rhythm until Chiara was biting down on her hand to stop herself from screaming out loud. Nico slammed into her and sent her body flying into an orgasm so intense she thought she might pass out.

He wasn't far behind her, and he collapsed over

her back, shuddering his release deep inside her for long moments.

After a few minutes he pulled free and turned her around. She was still dizzy.

'What do you *do* to me?' he asked hoarsely. 'I didn't intend on ravishing you in the pool, but I get near you and...'

She looked up at him, the aftershocks of pleasure still coursing through her system. 'I could say the same of you,' she said shakily.

It was in these brief moments, in the aftermath of pleasure, that there was some demolition of the wall between them. But soon Nico would recover and return to his cool, solicitous self. She could see it happening now. The raw, open look was fading from his face and he was stepping back.

She felt very naked—because she *was* naked, she realised. Her swimsuit was somewhere at the bottom of the pool.

Nico said, 'Stay here. I'll get you something.'

He waded out of the pool, his body gleaming, muscles rippling, and went up the steps, totally and unashamedly naked. He went into the small cabana by the pool, which held supplies, and when he re-emerged he had a towel hitched around his waist and was carrying a terrycloth robe for her.

He held it out at the top of the steps and Chiara crossed her arms over her breasts self-consciously. 'I can't walk out like this—what if someone sees?'

'They're all having dinner in the kitchen on the other side of the *castello*. I was just in there.'

Chiara glared at him. He was daring her. Something rebellious rose up within her—a wish to try and unsettle him, break him out of that cool, impersonal place he went back to whenever they'd been intimate.

So she waded out too, and went up the steps, aware of the water sluicing off her body, which still felt too sensitive.

Nico's eyes were dark by the time she reached the top, his mouth a tight line. She stood in front of him for a long moment, for once revelling in her nakedness.

Nico bitterly regretted goading Chiara. He should know by now that she was never to be underestimated. She stood before him like a beacon of fertile sensuality—heavy breasts, wide hips, her rotund belly carrying their child. And suddenly *he* was the one afraid of people looking out of a window and seeing her. He didn't want anyone else's eyes on her. *Ever.*

He put the robe around her shoulders, waited till she'd fed her arms through and then belted it firmly.

He might have thought she was unaware of her power over him—the insanity that consumed him until he was buried inside her and the world returned to sharp focus—but after watching her sashay up those steps like a fertile warrior goddess he knew better.

He could feel himself drawing back, to the place inside where he didn't feel so raw. He took a step away and saw some of the light in her green eyes fade. He ignored the pang in his chest. He didn't need that.

'Maria said dinner will be ready when we come in.'

Chiara forced down the frustration to see Nico so utterly in control again. 'Fine. I'll take a shower and clean up.'

Chiara watched as Nico strode back up the garden towards the *castello*. For a moment she could almost imagine he was one of his ancestors —a marauding Greek or Moor.

The truth was that Chiara wouldn't ever have got close to a man like Nico if it hadn't been for extraordinary circumstances. She was average in height, and looks, and was becoming more like a beached whale with every passing day.

Yet, remarkably, they still had insane chemistry. Which was all very well—for now. But what would happen when Nico's desire for her fizzled out, as it invariably would? And what would happen when the baby was born and they had to deal with a whole new reality? Babies tested the best of relationships.

Would she have the strength to keep up the pretence that she was okay with just this and not *more*? Or would the huge cracks that she knew were ever-expanding just below the surface of their relationship appear and tear them apart completely?

She couldn't imagine a man like Nico settling for life with a wife he no longer found attractive, and she wouldn't be able to bear it if he took mistresses.

She was going to have to talk to him. But while

the after-effects of his lovemaking still flowed through her blood like nectar she thought *Just not yet.*

A week later

Nico leant against the door that led outside from the kitchen, where a small vegetable and herb garden was laid out. Chiara was on her knees, planting something in the ground, wearing a huge sun hat to keep the sun off her face. Her hair was long and tangled down her back, and with irritating predictability all Nico wanted to do was go over, wrap her hair around his hand and tug her head back so she presented her lush mouth to him.

Irritating because he couldn't see an end to this desire that seemed to pulse through his system with growing force. Not less force. It wasn't that he didn't *want* to find his wife attractive, but her role as his wife of convenience wasn't meant to include making him feel insatiable lust.

At least if that diminished Nico might feel some semblance of control returning. Right now, control was an elusive concept.

She must have sensed his presence, because

she turned around and looked up. Her face was flushed and she smiled and Nico found it hard to breathe.

He said, '*What* are you wearing?'

The smile slid off her face and Nico could breathe again—but he felt like a heel.

'They're old dungarees belonging to my father. I thought they'd be perfect for doing some gardening.'

Nico couldn't take his eyes off her. She shouldn't have looked remotely sexy in a sleeveless vest and cut-off voluminous dungarees, but right then he was hard pushed to drum up a sexier image.

Chiara clambered to her feet, which were in bright pink flip-flops. Today her toenails were painted purple. Desire hit Nico directly in his solar plexus and moved down lower.

She said, 'Actually, I'm glad you're here—there's something I want to show you.'

Nico saw how flushed she was and said, 'When was the last time you drank some water?'

She blinked. 'Um…lunchtime?'

He made a disapproving noise and called back into the kitchen for some water. Maria came out with a bottle, clucking like a mother hen. Chiara took it and rolled her eyes at Nico before taking a few big gulps. It didn't help Nico to cool down when he saw drops dripping down her chin and under the neck of the T-shirt.

Dio. He was a walking hormone and *she* was the pregnant one. Pathetic.

'You said you wanted to show me something?'

She nodded and started to walk out of the small garden towards the area where the chapel and graveyards were situated. He stopped in his tracks when he saw that the old graveyard, full of his ancestors, had been completely cleared of foliage and that men were working on the gravestones, cleaning them and re-engraving them.

He could feel Chiara's eyes on him and his skin prickled.

'When did they start this?' His voice was sharp.

Chiara sounded nervous. 'When you went to Rome. I asked the landscape gardeners to look at it and one of them knows someone who cleans headstones. Do you mind?' she asked.

Nico felt as if a layer of skin was being peeled away to reveal the tender underside of a wound. It was disconcerting. 'Why would I mind? The truth is that it should never have been allowed to become overgrown in the first place.'

'No, it shouldn't,' she said quietly. 'And I thought that this would at least go some way to rectifying the situation.'

What Chiara had done cut right to the heart of him. Nico knew his reaction was irrational, but he couldn't control it—there was much he couldn't control at the moment. He felt as if his heart was expanding in his chest, cutting off all the oxygen, making it hard to breathe. He also— ridiculously—felt his eyes stinging.

All he could think of to counteract his reaction was to push Chiara back to where he might be able to breathe again.

He turned to her. 'Cleaning a graveyard won't do much to rectify the fact that your family wilfully denied us our home for generations. The only thing that *will* is when our daughter is born, and then a son, to breathe life back into the Santo Domenico name indelibly.'

Nico walked away from Chiara, but her stricken, hurt expression was burnt onto his brain. He told himself it was for the best. The sooner she remembered why they were married, the better.

* * *

'You haven't forgotten about the charity ball tonight in Naples? We'll be staying over, so you need to pack a bag.'

Chiara closed the book on pregnancy she'd been reading in the library and looked up. Hurt at the way Nico had reacted to the graveyard yesterday was still fresh in her stomach, making her feel ill, but she suppressed it.

'I've packed a bag. I'm ready to go when you are.'

He looked at his watch. 'We'll leave in an hour.'

Chiara didn't pick up her book again when he'd left. She couldn't concentrate. She rubbed her belly distractedly. The baby had been restless over the past few days. She figured it was just because she was getting closer and closer to her due date.

The cracks that she'd envisaged as being just below the surface of her marriage with Nico were becoming more apparent. And even though he'd shown her again and again that he wasn't ready to give *more*, that little kernel of hope inside her wouldn't die.

She hated herself for it, but sometimes she saw

an expression on Nico's face, or in his eyes, before he blanked it, that made her heart thump hard and made her think there might be a chance he could feel something for her.

But yesterday had been a brutal lesson in remembering her place. She had thought the restoration of the graveyard would please him, but maybe inadvertently she'd reminded him of his priorities.

She levered herself out of the chair to go and gather her things, telling herself that what she had to focus on was the baby—that had to be her priority for now, not wishing for things that would never happen.

Nico knew he was behaving like a boor, but he couldn't seem to help himself. They'd taken his private jet for the short flight to Naples, and he'd booked them into one of Naples's most exclusive hotels to get ready.

When Chiara had emerged from the dressing room he'd wanted to march her right back inside and peel the grey Grecian-style dress from her body. It was one-shouldered, and totally modest, but it seemed to cling indecently to every rounded curve.

She'd left her hair down and coiled it over one shoulder in a loose plait, and it glowed with brown and faint auburn highlights. She looked young and modern and fresh—and far too sexy for Nico's equilibrium.

He'd said nothing, though and they'd left, with the tension that had been between them since the graveyard incident yesterday still simmering. Nico knew he should apologise—Chiara was not to blame for the decisions made by her family many years ago, and he'd told her from the start that he didn't hold her personally responsible. And yet he couldn't bring himself to do it because he was afraid of the softening he'd see in those green eyes. He was afraid of how badly he wanted to see it. To have it soothe something ragged inside him.

When they'd arrived at the function he'd been cornered by some business associates who had been chasing him for weeks and Chiara had said, 'Go on—I'll find a drink and a seat.'

And now he couldn't see her, and frustration

was prickling over his skin. He was feeling claus-
trophobic.

And then finally he *did* spot her, over in the
corner, and hated how his heart-rate immediately
eased.

He kept her in his sights after that.

'Do you mind if I join you?'

Chiara looked up to see a tall and very elegant
grey-haired woman dressed in black hovering
over the chair beside her.

She put out a hand. 'Not at all. I'm afraid I'm
not being very sociable. High heels and swollen
ankles don't really mix very well.'

The woman sat down.

She looked familiar to Chiara, and she asked
impulsively, 'Have we met before?'

The woman shook her head. 'No, my dear, we
haven't. I'd remember you—you're one of the
most naturally beautiful women I've seen in these
circles in a long time.'

Chiara blushed, embarrassed by this compliment from a stranger. 'Thank you—what a nice
thing to say.'

The woman looked at her bump. 'Due soon?'

Chiara put a hand on her bump. 'In a couple of weeks. But I've been warned it could go over—most first babies do.'

Then the woman said, 'I'm sorry—how rude of me. I'm Patrizia Sorellani. Pleased to meet you.'

Chiara took her outstretched hand. 'Chiara Santo Domenico.'

The woman held on to her hand. 'You're married to Nicolo Santo Domenico?'

Chiara nodded. 'Yes. Do you know him?'

The women pulled her hand back and nodded. She looked sad. 'Yes, I do…in a way. I'm his mother.'

Chiara absorbed the shock. 'You knew who I was before you came over?'

The woman nodded unhappily. 'I'm sorry. I hope you don't mind. I've been trying to get him to meet me for some time now, but he keeps rebuffing me. I thought that maybe—'

'What are you doing here? You are not welcome.'

Both women looked up to see Nico towering over them. He was glaring at his mother in a way that Chiara recognised from their first meeting. She barely knew the other woman, but she knew instinctively what she should do—even though it would incur Nico's wrath.

She stood up. 'Your mother is here because she wants to speak with you.'

Nico turned his glare on Chiara, but she met it full-on.

'Can't you give her just five minutes?'

For what seemed like an aeon Nico said nothing, and then, finally, 'Very well. Five minutes. Come with me.'

He turned and stalked off. Patrizia turned to Chiara for a moment, saying emotionally, 'Thank you so much.' Then she hurried after her son.

Chiara sat down again, a little shell-shocked.

It was about fifteen minutes before Nico reappeared, and he looked grim.

Chiara put down her glass. 'What is it? Is everything okay?'

He took her arm. 'We're leaving.'

He all but marched her out of the function room to where his car was waiting outside. Once in the back of the car, and when it was moving Chiara said, 'How did it go with your mother? She seemed…nice…' she finished lamely.

Nico was looking out of the other window, his

whole form tense. 'I listened to what she had to say.'

'Nico—'

He turned to her. 'Something else has come up. I'm going to drop you at the hotel and then I'm going to fly to Rome tonight. The plane will return to take you home in the morning. I'll be back tomorrow evening.'

In other words he wasn't going to discuss his mother or whatever else was going on.

They were pulling up outside the hotel now. Nico got out and came around to let Chiara out of the car. He escorted her inside and left her at the lift. By the time she was in the suite and kicking off her shoes frustration was bubbling up inside her.

Maybe Nico did have a crisis to attend to— maybe he didn't. But one thing was clear: she was not welcome to stray out of the clear boundary zone he'd put her in all those months ago.

Chiara undressed and undid her hair, cleaned off her make-up. Then she pulled on a thick robe and went on to the outdoor balcony, leaning on the railing, drinking in the view of Naples at night, this thriving, hectic, chaotic city.

She sucked in a deep breath. It was time to face facts. Nico wasn't going to miraculously fall in love with her. He was going to continue to operate like a lone wolf and punish her for getting too close by shutting her out.

The future she faced was stark. It was also lonely. And Chiara needed to figure out what was best for her and her baby.

By the time Nico returned to the *castello* the following evening—late—Chiara was waiting. Nervous but composed. She had let all the staff have a night off, because there was a fête in the local village, so there would be no interruptions.

He came into the reception room and saw her straight away. 'You shouldn't have waited up.'

Chiara noticed that he looked tired and her silly heart clenched. His jaw was stubbled. 'Was everything okay?'

He moved over to the drinks cabinet, pulling at his tie as he did so. He poured himself a shot of whisky and downed it in one. And then he turned around.

'There was a fire at a tech plant I own outside Rome.'

Chiara gasped, and immediately felt guilty for having thought he was just trying to avoid her. 'Was anyone hurt?'

He shook his head. 'Thankfully there were no employees there—just security guards, and they raised the alarm. It'll be covered by insurance.'

Chiara said, 'You should have told me, Nico. I want to know when things like that happen.'

'But it's nothing to do with you.'

'Of course it is! I'm your *wife*.'

For a long moment he said nothing, and then he said, 'Fair enough. And I owe you an apology. I handled the graveyard thing badly. It was a shock to see it like that...exposed, and being taken care of, after all these years. I shouldn't have taken it out on you—you did a good thing.'

'I wanted to do a good thing. I never meant anything else. But maybe I should have asked first. After all, this isn't my home any more.'

He frowned. 'Yes, it is, Chiara—you're having my child.'

She felt desperation rise in the face of Nico's infuriating calm. This was what he did—retreated to that civil place. No emotion.

'But it's not really my home, is it? I'm here

mainly under sufferance—because you didn't want to wait until the *castello* was in the bank's hands and I didn't want to let it go. And then I got pregnant. We both know I wouldn't be here if it weren't for that sequence of events.' She continued painfully, 'I know you wouldn't throw me out…but I'll never be anything more than a glorified guest.'

'What are you talking about?'

'I'm talking about the fact that you are determined to shut me out at all costs, Nico. Whenever I stray too close you push me away. And I know you told me you can't ever give me *more*, and I know I thought I could deal with that, but the fact is… I can't.'

He just looked at her.

Chiara kept going before she lost her nerve.

'The truth is that I fell in love with you, Nico, way back… I think on our wedding night. And when you were so clinical the next morning, so unmoved, I realised that I had it all wrong. It had just been a physical thing for you, while for me…it changed my life. *Me*. I was so terrified you'd notice that I ran away, hoping I'd never see you again. But then I became pregnant. And you brought me back.

'Even then I tried to tell myself it wasn't love. That it was infatuation because you'd been my first lover. But it wasn't. I *love* you, Nico, and I do want more, and I won't survive with you unless you can give me that… So I think the best thing, once the baby comes, is if I move somewhere else. We can talk about custody arrangements at a later date.'

She finished speaking and felt her heart beating wildly. Nico looked stunned. As if someone had just punched him.

'Why are you telling me you love me? Is it because you're hoping it might get you back on the deeds of the *castello*? Is that what this is all about?'

Chiara should have known to expect Nico's ever-present cynicism, but it was still a shock.

She shook her head. 'No, it's not about me trying to get anything. It's about self-preservation.'

His eyes were burning. 'You're having my child. You can't leave.'

Chiara tipped up her chin. She felt as if her insides were being lacerated, and there was a dull pain at the base of her spine. 'Nico, after the baby is born I'm going to ask for a divorce.'

He shook his head and put the glass in his hand down with a clatter on the drinks tray. 'Chiara, this is crazy. You know what we have...'

He started walking towards her and panic galvanised Chiara into action. If he touched her she'd crumble.

She put up her hand. 'Please—don't. I don't want you, Nico. Not like that. Not now.'

Liar. You'll always want him.

She saw that look in his eye—the look that told her he was thinking that all he had to do was touch her and she'd acquiesce.

Her panic intensified. 'I'm sleeping alone tonight, Nico. I need some space.'

The intense expression on his face and in his eyes faded, to be replaced with the mask Chiara recognised well.

She was doing the right thing. She had to do this.

The tone in Nico's voice when he spoke was ominous. 'We'll talk in the morning.'

Chiara had said her piece and now just wanted to escape, so she could lick her wounds. She left

Nico behind in the reception room and went up to the bedroom. The pain in her back had intensified and she was feeling crampy. She put it down to emotional stress and got ready for bed.

It was when she was about to get into bed that the first crippling spasm of pain hit her—right across her belly. It was so strong she couldn't breathe for a long moment. When it had passed she gasped for air, and it was only then that she noticed she was wet. She looked down and for a horrific moment thought she'd wet herself, But then she realised what it was and said wonderingly, 'My waters have broken...'

A wholly different kind of panic surged as reality set in and Chiara rushed out of the bedroom, cold and clammy. She went back down to the reception room, but Nico wasn't there. He wasn't in the study either.

By now Chiara was sweating, and she felt another wave of pain about to hit. She doubled over at the bottom of the stairs, groaning. This spasm was longer and more painful. She was also feeling an urge to push, which terrified her.

She forced herself to breathe deeply and calmly as she checked all the bedrooms, and she was almost giving up hope when she saw a light coming from under the door leading to the gym that Nico had had installed. She pushed open the door and he was there, dressed in sweats, punching a bag with a ferocity she'd never seen him exhibit before.

She collapsed to her knees as another contraction hit and Nico saw her. He threw off his gloves and rushed over, crouching down.

She gripped him and got out, 'Waters broken… contractions…the baby is coming.'

He looked at her stupidly for a moment, and as the contraction died away Chiara gripped his hand.

'This is what happened to my mother, Nico. She had me here at the *castello*…then there were complications…she couldn't have any more children… I'm scared.'

Nico rose to his feet in a smooth movement, lifting her into his arms. He said grimly, 'That won't happen. I'm going to put you in the car and take you to the hospital.'

Chiara could feel the next contraction coming and said urgently, 'There's no time, Nico. She's coming... I need to push. You have to call an ambulance—they'll tell you what to do.'

After Nico had laid her down on the bed he got someone on the end of the phone—a paramedic—and it all became a blur to Chiara. She was in the grip of an elemental force and just had to hang on for dear life.

All she could do was focus on Nico and do as he told her to do. After what felt like hours of excruciating pain she felt a rush of energy between her legs—a great release—and then she had an image of Nico's awestruck face as he held his tiny daughter in his hands. There was an impression of flashing lights before she slipped into blessed darkness and relief from pain.

CHAPTER TEN

'I'M VERY HAPPY to be able to tell you, Signora Santo Domenico, that all is well. There is no reason why you can't go home tomorrow.'

Chiara couldn't stop the knot of anxiety tightening inside her even though she held her perfect sleeping baby in her arms. 'There were no complications?'

The hospital doctor glanced at Nico, who was also in the room. 'Your husband did tell me what happened to your mother, but, no, happily things have moved on from those days, and there is nothing to worry about. You had a textbook birth—thanks to your husband—and the only reason you fainted was because of pain and shock.' He patted her hand reassuringly and said, 'I'll come back later to check on you, but please don't worry. Everything is fine.'

Chiara forced a smile and felt relief wash through her. She knew that everything *wasn't* fine, though. She had told Nico that she loved him and it hadn't precipitated a declaration of anything from him except that she couldn't leave. She could still recall finding him in the gym, punching that bag with all his might...

'Chiara...'

She looked at Nico reluctantly. He was still in his sweats, hair messy.

'You should go home, Nico.' Her conscience pricked. 'Thank you for what you did—you were amazing. I don't know what I would have done if you hadn't been there.'

His face darkened. 'I'm your *husband*, dammit, you don't have to thank me. It was the most profound experience of my life.'

Chiara's heart clenched. She could still recall seeing the awestruck look on Nico's face just before she'd lost consciousness. She'd never seen that look before.

'Chiara, we need to talk.'

She shook her head, not at all ready for their inevitable conversation. 'I'm tired, Nico. Go home. We can talk another time...'

He looked obstinate for a moment, as if he

was going to refuse, but then he sighed and said, 'Fine, I'll come back later.'

Chiara wanted to tell him not to, but he was already walking out of the room. When he was gone she turned her head away from the door and let a tired tear slip out of her eye.

These last few hours had been a rollercoaster, and she needed to conserve her strength if she was going to do battle with a man who wanted to insist they stay together even though he didn't love her, and who would use his seductive wiles to manipulate her.

She turned her attention to their daughter and let a rush of maternal love and gratitude for her healthy baby distract from everything.

When Chiara woke later that day she opened her eyes and automatically checked the cot beside the bed—but it was empty. She lifted her head, panic gripping her for a moment.

But then she saw where her daughter was and blinked. And blinked again. She was cradled in Nico's arms, and one of his fingers was clutched in a tiny fist. He'd obviously gone home and showered and changed. His hair was still damp and he wore jeans and a polo shirt, and he looked gorgeous.

There was a look of such naked wonder and awe on his face that Chiara almost felt like a voyeur. Still raw after the birth, she had no defence for seeing Nico like this, with their baby. No defence for the evidence that he *could* feel emotion. Clearly he was in love. Just not with Chiara. And it shamed her that she felt jealous.

She wondered if perhaps she'd been too hasty. Surely if he could love their daughter then she had a duty to try and make their marriage work?

He must have heard her move because he looked up and caught her eye. Immediately his expression blanked. And Chiara knew in that moment that she wasn't strong enough to do it. To spend a lifetime with a man who didn't love her. No matter how much he might love their daughter.

All Nico could see was Chiara's bright green gaze. It left him nowhere to hide, and he wondered if she had witnessed the moment when his heart had swelled so much he'd almost been afraid it would burst, as he looked down at the fragile perfection of his daughter.

Catching her tiny slithery fragile body in his

hands when she'd been born had been a truly magical experience—which had turned to one of sheer horror when he'd realised that Chiara wasn't conscious.

He never wanted to go through that stomach-curdling feeling of terror again. He'd lived and died a hundred deaths in those moments as he'd knelt there, holding the exquisite miracle of his daughter, while also contemplating the bone-numbing terror of Chiara's unmoving body.

All the emotions he'd shut off for years had come bursting out of his heart, cracking it open and blasting down the walls he'd erected around it to keep himself safe for years. He'd been an idiot to think he could hold back the dam which had been building inside him from the moment he'd laid eyes on Chiara Caruso.

A God he hadn't acknowledged for a long time had kept Chiara safe. And his daughter. And had answered his fevered prayers.

Feeling more raw than he had ever felt in his life, Nico stood up with Sofia and took her over to Chiara. He desperately felt the need to articulate what was inside him, but didn't know where to start.

As he handed Sofia into Chiara's arms he said, 'Chiara...'

But she looked up at him and said, 'I need to feed her and then change her.' She looked down again, dismissing him.

Her words were like a slap. It reminded him painfully of the day when he'd come to the *castello* to proposition her. When she'd held his card in her hand and refused to meet his eye. He could see now that that had been the moment when she'd touched something much deeper inside him than mere intrigue. He'd been fooling himself all along.

He tried again. 'Chiara...'

She looked up. Her face was expressionless. 'We're fine. You should go. It's late.'

Nico felt a very uncharacteristic sense of defeat. He'd met his equal in Chiara, there was no doubt about that. But he also felt a sense of renewed purpose. Now came the most difficult part. Convincing Chiara to listen to him. And, more, to *believe* him.

The next day Chiara was let out of hospital with Sofia. Nico took them home in a brand-new family-friendly car, with a newly installed baby seat in the back, where Chiara sat beside Sofia to keep an eye on her.

She knew that sooner or later they'd have to talk. When she felt stronger, she told herself weakly.

When they returned to the *castello* Chiara felt ridiculously emotional to see all the staff lined up to greet them. Maria was beaming and clucked over Sofia, and even the gardeners looked suspiciously dewy-eyed.

Spiro, faithful as ever, just came up and nudged Chiara's thigh, telling her he was there. She had noticed that he would invariably gravitate to Nico's study if she wasn't around, and she'd often find him there curled up under the table.

Chiara took Sofia up to the nursery they'd set up directly across the hall from the master bedroom. It was a beautiful sunny room, with brightly coloured furniture and murals on the walls. She stopped in the doorway when she saw the new additions. Stuffed toys of every description were dotted around the room and in the cot, and there was a gorgeous upholstered rocking chair with a foot-rest and wide arms, perfect for nursing.

She could sense Nico behind her and asked faintly, 'Did you do this?'

He sounded wary. 'I just got a few extra things.'

His thoughtfulness made her feel vulnerable, and she knew she wasn't strong enough to look at him, so she half turned and said, 'Thank you, they're lovely. I'm going to change Sofia and feed her now—can you give us some privacy?'

There was a taut moment, and Chiara almost lost her nerve, but then Nico said, 'Sure,' and shut the door.

Chiara felt awful, and hated herself for feeling awful. But she *had* to shut Nico out of these tender, vulnerable moments or she would break completely.

'Chiara…wake up.'

Chiara's eyes flew open and she sat up. The chair rocked, pitching her forward.

Nico caught her, holding her by the arms. 'You were asleep. Maria will have dinner ready in half an hour, and I've run you a bath.'

Chiara looked over to the cot to see Sofia sleeping peacefully. 'Sofia—'

'Is fine,' Nico said firmly. 'I burped her and changed her.'

Chiara was suddenly wide awake. 'You did all that?'

'Maria showed me how.' He held up a baby monitor. 'We'll hear her if she needs anything.'

Chiara felt a pang. *She* should have been the one to show Nico how to care for Sofia and she couldn't believe she'd slept through it. She realised she was still in the clothes she'd worn home from the hospital, and also that she was starving. She felt thoroughly dishevelled.

Assuring herself that Sofia was fine, she followed Nico into the master bathroom, where a fragrant steaming bath was waiting. Chiara wanted to dive in and never come out again.

He closed the door and Chiara saw that he had laid out clean clothes—soft leggings, a long, loose cashmere top and underwear. Comfortable clothes. *Thoughtful.*

She sank into the bath, groaning in appreciation as the warm water soothed the parts of her that were still tender after giving birth.

She would have fallen asleep again if it hadn't been for Nico knocking on the door a short time later.

After washing, she got out and changed, not wanting to admit that she felt like a new woman. She avoided Nico's eye and tried not to notice how gorgeous he looked dressed in dark trousers and a long-sleeved top.

He led her downstairs after she'd checked again on Sofia, who was still sleeping soundly, her rosebud mouth in a little moue. Her lashes were long and dark. Taking after her father.

Maria served up a delicious hearty Sicilian stew, and it was only when Chiara sat back, replete and relaxed, that she saw the calculating gleam in Nico's eye and realised how cunningly he'd manipulated her.

'Chiara…we have to talk.'

She immediately tensed. 'We have nothing to talk about.'

He fixed her with those dark eyes so like his daughter's. 'We have *everything* to talk about.'

Chiara felt panic rise. She stood up and put down her napkin. 'I don't want to do this now.'

He put out a hand. 'Okay, let me just tell you

about my mother, can I? I couldn't tell you that night because it was a lot to process, and in all honesty I had trouble articulating it even to myself...'

Chiara sat down again, reluctant but curious. She hadn't expected him to mention his mother. 'Okay...'

Nico sighed. 'She told me that night at the party about why she left. She had suffered from a mild form of bipolar disorder since her teens. When she got pregnant with me it exacerbated the condition and she couldn't take her medication. My father was unsympathetic, not understanding mental illness. By the time my mother gave birth she was terrified she was going to do something drastic, like run away with me. She knew enough to know she couldn't do that to me, so she left—and left me behind. She told me that she came back a couple of years later, when she was stable again, but my father refused to hear her explanation. He said she had shamed him and he told her to leave and never come back.'

Chiara couldn't stop her heart aching for Nico and his mother. 'I'm so sorry...'

Nico shook his head. 'I always blamed her,

but it was my father who refused to give her a chance. She had no money, no resources to try and mount a legal battle—and anyway, they would have made mincemeat of her in a court once they knew about her illness. So she left and got on with her life... But she told me she never forgot about me. She sent me letters but they never reached me—my father must have destroyed them.'

Chiara curled her hand into a fist to stop herself from reaching out to touch Nico. 'I'm glad you know now. Are you going to see her again?'

He nodded. 'Yes, at some stage. But it's thanks to you, for pushing me to listen to her...otherwise I would have cut her off again.'

Chiara shook her head. 'I'm sure you would have listened to her eventually.'

Feeling even more vulnerable after hearing about Nico's mother, Chiara put down her napkin. She was about to make her excuses and leave when Nico said, 'Wait, I need to say something else.'

She stopped, her heart pounding. She desperately wanted to escape Nico's inexorable pull, but she forced herself to ask. 'What?'

'I love you.'

He was looking directly at her, his eyes never darker or more intense.

Chiara couldn't breathe. 'What did you say?'

His jaw clenched. 'I said, I love you.'

A surge of hope so strong that it made her tremble, galvanised Chiara to move up and away from the table. Out of Nico's orbit.

She hugged herself. She couldn't believe this… the risk was too great. He'd told her about his mother just to play on her emotions. He had too much to lose now if she insisted on divorcing him. He loved his daughter. Of course he was going to do his utmost to convince her otherwise.

'You don't have to say this just because I said it to you, Nico.'

He stood up. 'I'm not. I mean it.'

Chiara shook her head, refusing to allow herself to believe. 'What we went through the night Sofia was born… You delivered her into your own hands. It's natural to associate strong emotions with an intense experience like that.'

'Don't patronise me, Chiara. I know what I feel.'

She desisted from reminding him that he'd said

more or less the same thing to her about losing her virginity.

'Then it's very convenient that you had this revelation *after* I told you I want a divorce and after the birth of your daughter—which is perhaps making you realise more than ever that you want to promote a united family front to your peers.'

He shook his head. 'You didn't used to be cynical.'

Chiara responded tartly, 'I wasn't, until I met *you.*'

She stopped and bit her lip. He was right, damn him. This wasn't like her.

'I'm tired, Nico. I'm going to bed. Sofia will be awake again for a feed shortly.' She stopped at the door and looked back. 'I'd appreciate it if I could sleep alone. I'll take Sofia into the bedroom in her Moses basket...'

Nico's jaw clenched visibly, but then he said, 'Of course. I'll sleep in a guest suite.'

As she went upstairs she told herself she was doing the right thing. Nico was ruthless—she'd seen it at first-hand. He wasn't above doing whatever it took to get what he wanted...even telling her he loved her.

* * *

When Chiara woke at dawn the next morning she found a note on the pillow beside hers. She picked it up, recognising the slashing writing instantly.

Chiara,
I have to go to Rome on business for a couple
of days. We will talk again when I get back.
Nico

An incredible sense of disappointment flooded her. She'd refused to believe Nico last night, but she'd woken with that eternal flame of hope inside her, and before she'd seen the note she'd thought to herself that if he said it again...tried to convince her...she might just believe him.

But she'd been right. Evidently he'd given up the pretence and gone back to work. Maybe he was with his solicitors right now, drawing up papers for their divorce?

Just then Sofia awoke, making small mewling sounds, and Chiara reached over and plucked her out of the Moses basket, plumping up the pillows behind her so she could get comfortable for feeding. As Sofia latched on to Chiara's breast with unerring accuracy and suckled strongly Chiara once again reminded herself that the most important thing was this small baby, and protecting her from whatever fallout lay ahead.

Nico looked across the lawn to where Chiara was lying in the shade on a sunbed, with Sofia in a pram beside her and another umbrella shading her. She was wearing a strapless swimsuit and she'd never looked more beautiful.

He felt an incredible sense of vulnerability and trepidation. It this didn't work he truly didn't know what he would do—for the first time in his life.

Chiara was drowsing in the late-afternoon sun when she sensed Nico's presence. Just like that. For the first time since she'd given birth there was a stirring deep inside her, and the small hairs stood up on her arms. She opened her eyes and saw he was approaching where she lay, looking fiercely determined.

She scrambled up to a sitting position, pulling a shawl across her bare shoulders.

'Nico. You're back.' He must have been back for a while, because he was dressed in worn jeans and a loose shirt. Rolled-up sleeves. Hair damp from the shower.

He sat down on the lounger beside hers. Too close. Chiara couldn't breathe for a moment. She wasn't ready to see him. He'd caught her unawares.

'I said we'd talk when I got back.'

Chiara scooted back nervously. 'Sofia is due a feed…she'll wake in a minute.'

'Stop using our daughter as a defence, Chiara. I'm just asking you to listen to me for a few minutes—is that too much to ask?'

There was a bleak tone to Nico's voice that she hadn't heard before and she went still. 'No, of course not.'

He relaxed marginally and Chiara realised how tense he was.

He ran a hand through his hair and muttered something like, *'God, this is hard.'* Then he looked at her. 'I told you I loved you the other evening. And I meant it.'

Chiara opened her mouth but he put up a hand.

'No. Let me finish. I can appreciate that you might not believe me, given the nature of why and how we married. Given the fact that I've done my best to keep you at a distance… But the truth is that I didn't know how to let you get close. And every time you did it repelled me—because that's how I deal with *any* kind of intimacy. My father never showed me affection. My relationship with Alexandra was immature and incredibly selfish. I thought I loved her, so I associated being betrayed with being in love. It took seeing her again—next to you—for me to realise that I'd felt nothing for her. She wounded my ego, nothing else.

'I think that's when I fell in love with you—not that I was ready to admit that then. No one had ever defended me before, until you literally stepped in front of me and confronted her. But I wasn't ready to admit to any feelings other than *like* and *respect*. That's what I told myself when I laid out the reasons why I thought this marriage could work.

'I knew you wanted more, Chiara, and on some level I think I knew you were in love with me. But in my arrogance I thought that was a *good* thing—you feeling more for me than I did for you. Which was a joke, because while I was telling myself you loved me I was falling for you and not even aware of it. All I knew was that if I left here for more than two days I had to get back. I couldn't contemplate desiring another woman ever again. I couldn't understand how my desire for you got stronger and stronger...why I was falling deeper and deeper.

'You did beautiful things—like the graveyard, and forcing me to confront my mother. But the emotions you stirred terrified me. It was easier to push you away. So I can understand why you won't believe me when I say *I love you.*' He sighed heavily. 'And, yes, it *did* take Sofia's birth and the terror of thinking I'd lost you to make me finally come to my senses... I needed to almost lose you to find my heart...'

Chiara was stunned into speechlessness. Nico drew a rolled-up sheaf of papers out of his back pocket and handed it to her. She went clammy at the thought that it was divorce papers. That he might have given up on hoping he could convince her.

She said, 'Nico—'

He put up a hand. 'Just take a look before you say anything.'

She unrolled the papers and it took a second

for her eyes to make out the ornate calligraphy. Slowly she said, 'These are the deeds to the *castello*...in the Caruso name.' She looked at him, not understanding.

'I needed to do something to convince you. The *castello* is back in your name. It's yours. I couldn't care less any more about my claim on it, because it's just bricks and mortar. What I care about is here in this garden, not on those deeds.'

And then he pulled a small box out of his jeans pocket. Chiara saw that his hands were trembling. He opened the box and revealed a plain gold band inlaid with tiny glittering emeralds.

'It's an eternity ring. Because I want to spend the rest of my life with you, Chiara, being your husband, partner, lover. I want to take you to all those cities and show you the world...'

Chiara was overwhelmed. She shook her head. 'I don't....' She couldn't speak. Her throat was too tight with emotion.

She saw Nico's face fall, the light in his eyes fade. He closed the velvet box and put it down before standing up. She realised that he was misreading her reaction.

'I'm sorry, Chiara, I never meant to hurt you.

If you still truly want a divorce then you can have it.'

He had turned to walk away before Chiara could make her body work. She stood up and called out hoarsely, 'Stop!'

Nico stopped, his back to her.

She started towards him, her legs like jelly. 'You didn't let me finish...'

He turned around and she saw the pain etched into his features. She took a deep shaky breath. 'What I was going to say was that I don't know what to say—except I love you with all my heart, and, yes, I want to spend the rest of my life with you too...'

The dawning relief on Nico's face told Chiara better than anything just how much he'd been holding back for so long. She wasn't sure who moved, but they were in each other's arms, mouths fused in a desperate kiss of love and reunion.

When they broke apart Chiara looked up in wonder and traced Nico's mouth with a shaking finger. 'I love you so much. You deserve to be happy, Nico.'

His eyes were suspiciously bright. '*You* are my

happiness—you and Sofia. I love you both. For ever.'

Chiara looked deep into Nico's eyes and saw his soul reflecting back all the passion and emotion he'd been denying himself. She took a deep breath and allowed herself to believe. *Really* believe.

As if reading her mind, he said, 'You deserve to be happy too, *cara*.'

She smiled tremulously and nodded. 'I am—finally.'

Just then a mewling cry sounded from the pram and they both smiled.

Nico traced Chiara's jaw and whispered, 'Later, *mio amore*, I'll show you just how much I love you...'

Chiara took Nico's hand and led him to where the pram sat in the shade. She took Sofia out, and as she nursed their daughter Nico picked up her hand and placed the eternity ring on her finger. He pressed a kiss to her hand before interlacing their fingers and letting the peace that had eluded him his whole life infuse every bone in his body.

He'd never believed in love...but now it was all he could see.

EPILOGUE

CHIARA FELT ARMS slide around her midriff from behind and the intimate contact of her husband's hard body against her back as he settled behind her and stretched his legs alongside hers, where she sat on the sand in the shade.

As it always did without fail, her pulse sped up and her body reacted to his proximity. She leant back against him, letting him take her weight. She sighed happily. 'You're home.'

'I told you I'd make it back before dinner.'

She craned her head to look at him. 'You're not missing the buzz of Rome or New York too much?'

Nico had moved his main office from Rome to Syracuse, and he commuted in and out of there every day now—apart from the occasions when he had to go abroad, when he invariably took Chiara with him.

'It's the only thing that keeps me sane, having you near me,' he'd told her.

'No way,' he said now.

Chiara felt his voice running through her body like a happy hum of contentment. She'd never have guessed he could smile so much, or laugh, but that was all he seemed to do these days.

'Did you speak to your mother?'

She could feel him nod—yes. 'She's coming at the weekend.'

'Good.' Chiara was happy for Nico that he and his mother had developed a relationship at last. Patrizia adored visiting and spending time with them.

Nico's lips feathered a kiss near her ear and he asked, 'Well, is this close to what you imagined all those years ago?'

Chiara had told him of her fantasies about the kind of life she'd wanted at the *castello*. She looked around them and smiled. Sometimes her heart felt too full, as if it would burst. Now was one of those moments, on the small beach she'd always loved so much.

Their eldest daughter Sofia was holding one-year-old Luca by the hand and encouraging him to walk in the shallows of the sea. He was squealing with delight every time a small wave washed over his feet and pudgy legs. He had a head full of thick dark hair, and sometimes he reminded her so much of Nico that it hurt.

The twins, Alicia and Alessandro, were building sandcastles nearby under an umbrella, their hair almost blonde from the sun, freckles dusting their cheeks. They both had the green eyes of their mother, while Sofia and Luca had dark brown eyes.

Happy sounds and splashing water filled the air. She nodded against Nico's chest, feeling emotional. 'This doesn't even come close…it's so much better.'

Nico laced his hands with hers and squeezed tight. 'I didn't even have this dream—you gave it to me.'

Chiara tipped her head back and Nico pressed a kiss to her mouth. It held the promise of passion to come and endless love.

And just then came an excited squeal from Alicia, '*Papa!* You're home!'

Chiara felt Nico smile against her mouth as the moment turned into happy chaos and four children aged from six to one, descended upon their parents and buried them under a sea of legs, arms and kisses.

As the sun set on the small beach Nico and Chiara gathered up their family and made their way home to the *castello*. The stone above the main entrance now read *Castello Santo Domenico Caruso*, reflecting what was on the deeds.

They passed by the two graveyards, old and new. They were one graveyard now—two families united by love in the end.

* * * * *

LET'S TALK

Romance

For exclusive extracts, competitions
and special offers, find us online:

f facebook.com/millsandboon

⊙ @millsandboonuk

🐦 @millsandboon

Or get in touch on 0844 844 1351*

For all the latest titles coming soon,
visit millsandboon.co.uk/nextmonth